T0114912

Danjoo, a Miracle Child

by

Yaya Sillah

Also by the author

This is a work of fiction. Names, characters, businesses, places, events, locales, and incidents are either the products of the author's imagination or used in a fictitious manner. Any resemblance to actual persons, living or dead, or actual events is purely coincidental.

We publish books in the pursuit of human advancement
Visit our website at www.subakunda.com
Email: subakunda@yahoo.com
Mobile: +2209459540
Address: Kotu West K.M.C, The Gambia

ISBN: 979-8-6119-5097-5

Published 2023

Cover image credit: profile_veneratio at 123RF.com

In this materialistic world, when logic and common sense are absent, superstition and vanity will thrive above ethics and morality. Thus, man's infinite love for power and glory often dictates his character and wisdom. Moreover, in a multi-cultural society, the moment that you think you know everything is the time that you need to go back to school and learn more. The saying goes "You don't know your lover until you let her go", yet in a love triangle, you know your lover only when you are not competing to win her back.

Danjoo, a miracle child, totally disagrees with such a notion. However, let's travel deep into the wilderness in order to determine whether he is right or wrong.

1

My name is Abdul, but some people call me Charlie. I'm a cab driver, originally from Uttar Pradesh in India. I live in Hounslow with my wife and four children. I work 12 hours every day from 12 p.m. until midnight, six days a week. In the past 25 years I made enough money to buy three properties in Hounslow. However, Uber is making life a living hell for most drivers in the city now, and we struggle to make ends meet. Lately I've often thought about quitting cabbing and starting a new business, but I wonder if it is really worth starting something new, bearing in mind that a few years ago my two daughters graduated from university, one with a masters degree in finance and the other with a PhD in medicine, and each of them has an impressive salary. Also my two sons will graduate from university next year, hence at 55, do I still have to carry on working like a new arrival from India or shall I just retire now and rest until death is upon me?

While I lived in this limbo, one November evening, the London sky battered the city with heavy rain like a fireman quenching a raging fire with his hose. Despite that, it was business as usual, and I dropped off one passenger and picked up another until about 11:30 p.m. I was about to finish my shift, riding on Romford Road from Mile End towards the city. I was alone in the car and enjoying some Indian music. As I approached Whitechapel, I saw a hand in the darkness, waving at me to stop. I indicated, stopped and a man jumped into the car.

It had been a while since I last drove for a handsome white guy like him.

He was tall and bald-headed, wearing glasses and carrying a briefcase, dressed in a blue suit and white shirt. He was very smart indeed and he leant back in the vehicle like he owned it. I could only compare him to one of those high profile guys in Davos and he was as comfortable in my cab as if it was his own private car.

I accelerated off towards Central London. After a short pause, a great conversation between us started.

"Can you kindly drive me to Birmingham? I need to meet someone urgently and the last train has departed," he said. "And if you don't mind, if you switch off your radio, I have a fascinating story to share with you."

I did exactly as he requested. I was strangely excited to hear what he had to say. He started talking to me in a soft voice, like a primary school teacher to a student.

***

Ten years ago, in this multi-cultural city of London, for many centuries, people from different backgrounds lived side by side in peace and harmony as one community. Despite trials and tribulations, nonetheless, nothing shook the foundations of our community cohesion. Individual ethnic groups had a tendency to live by their own distinct way of life, but all the inhabitants of the city were equal before the law. Regardless of its metropolitan challenges in terms of marriage and family life, each individual group would usually follow their own beliefs and tradition, despite some customs and norms which were more peculiar then others.

In Canning Town, East London, a promising young lad of 25 years, Joseph, who was a telecommunication engineer working for BT in Canada Water, and the eloquent Grace, a 21 year old hotel receptionist working for Ibis in Central London, got married in a local church. Three months earlier, the bride's father Alexander had passed away in Romania and as a result the wedding was a low key event. Two days after the wedding, Grace moved in with Joseph at his parent's house. Joseph and Grace belonged to the same social class. They were both born in London, however their parents came from Eastern Europe, and were close friends. Though the pair had only seen each other twice before and had not talked to each other before their first date, the couple got married the following week. In their tradition it was compulsory for a newly wedded husband to pay his wife a dowry in gold equivalent to £12,000. However, if she failed to conceive a child by their first anniversary, then she would be deemed inadequate to make a family. Under such awkward circumstances the groom is legally entitled to claim back half of the dowry in order for him to marry a second wife. On the other hand, if she is lucky enough to conceive within one year after their wedding and she gives birth to a baby girl, then the wife would be entitled to retain the full amount of her dowry. In addition to that she will be the king maker in the family.

But if the child is a boy, then the husband is in charge. In the event of an extra martial affair, whoever is caught cheating in the marriage would be obliged to pay the other a penalty of not less than £2000. However, if the wife is caught cheating on her husband more than twice, she will lose all her rights as a wife and become a virtual slave to him for the rest of her life. Equally if he is caught cheating on her for more than twice, then he would be a mere servant in the house without the right to ever get married again.

A few weeks into their union, Joseph and Grace pushed their marriage into a high gear. Paris, a city which is known for its romantic life, was the first destination for their honeymoon. Then the couple continued to explore their passion from one hot spot to another across Europe. They partied in Barcelona, Venice and Rome. Finally, after three weeks of exploring Europe, Joseph and Grace returned home exhausted but carried on partying every weekend in London. Frankly from the outset, there was no doubt that these two party animals were deep in love. Since their wedding they could not get enough of each other. Each weekend Joseph and Grace would invite their friends to party with them like there was no tomorrow.

Joseph didn't care what other people thought about their relationship: all that mattered to him was Grace. However, they both knew that they should have a child before their first anniversary. At a dinner party with their friends, Joseph joked "Should that be so difficult for a 25 year old man and a 21 year old woman?"

"I don't think so, honey." Grace replied. Everyone laughed. "We just want live in the here and now and enjoy ourselves, don't we?"

"I don't give a damn about the future!" Joseph confirmed.

But their extravagant lifestyle began to raise eyebrows among the people in their social circle, and Grace's best friend Precious decided to alert the couple.

One Tuesday afternoon during their lunch break, Precious took Grace for a drink. She sat opposite Grace at the bar and to break the ice, started to make jokes about her own new hairstyle. They sipped their hot coffee, chatted, and were really having great time in the bar. After a few more giggles together, Precious got a little more serious.

"Grace, I really admire you and Joseph. You guys look like soul mates. It seems like a match made in heaven and wow, it's really amazing how you support each other. I wish I could have a loving husband like yours. But don't you feel it's time to make a few changes? I realise that you two like to have fun all the time but you spend a fortune on food and designer clothes, which are all fine, but don't you think it's time to grow up? Please don't get me wrong: I'm not jealous. But I feel like I have to ask you this.

You both have some amazing qualities: you don't smoke, you don't do drugs or drink alcohol, however, it's quite obvious that you will have to be a mother pretty soon. Why don't you and Joseph starting to save money and plan for your future? Joseph's parents might find it difficult to accommodate you any longer, they are both quite old, and don't you think that maybe you are bothering them? It's almost three months since you were married and you are still living with your in-laws! Are you guys crazy? Don't you think it's time for you and Joseph to buy your own property and move out?"

Grace got the wrong end of the stick, lashed out in a rage and yelled at Precious.

"Oh you silly girl! Stop being so horrible. What are you talking about? It's unbelievable. Are you jealous of me and our happiness? I don't care what you think and I don't care what anyone else thinks. We shall enjoy ourselves as much as we can. I am not taking orders from such a stupid friend as you!"

She angrily left the scene and left Precious sitting alone and embarrassed at the bar, disgusted at Grace's unreasonable behaviour. Finishing her coffee, she left the bar and went home.

Grace had ruined her relationship with her best friend, but when she got home later that evening, she couldn't wait to share the whole saga with her husband.

"Guess what, Joseph? Precious made some ridiculous remarks at work today."

"What did she say?"

"She was moaning about why we are living at your parents and blah blah blah... basically, she was trying to bully me and I lost my temper, then I stormed out of the bar and went straight back to work and left her there wondering. She is a loser."

"Darling, I told you from the start that she is jealous. She is almost 23 years old and still single; she can't even find a decent boyfriend." said Joseph. "Precious and my boss have the same attitude. They are extremely envious when they see us being happy. My boss was very critical of me too last week. Since we got married, from day one he is always nagging at me, but it has got worse, particularly in the past two weeks. He goes on and on. Last time he comes up to me and says 'Oh Joseph, lately you are late for work, and you seem distracted. You are always talking to your wife on the phone and you failed to attend our conference in Birmingham. I am warning you, if you continue behaving this way, very soon you are going to lose your job.'

Grace snorted. "Honey, let's jump on the next available flight to Las Vegas, and after that let's go to Dubai. That will make them feel even more jealous. Book five nights for us to stay in Vegas and then when we get back next weekend, we can also fly to Dubai to celebrate my 22nd birthday. That will give them a heart attack. What do you think?"

"Of course, darling, it's a great idea. You meant the world to me I truly want makes you feel special. Don't worry about the expense, I will take care of it. I'll book it tomorrow."

Grace was overwhelmed with joy, as she gallivanted like a clumsy teenager, hugging and kissing Joseph. "Thank you, honey!"

Joseph kept his promise. The next day he booked five extravagant nights in Las Vegas. Three days later the couple flew there via New York, and once in the city, they followed their usual pattern: an expensive hotel, designer clothes, and delicious food. However, on this particular trip, the couple added clubbing and gambling to their menu.

The exuberant couple happily spent the first couple of nights clubbing in down-town Vegas and then they gambled at various locations across the city. Amazingly, at one casino the lucky couple won a whopping $20,000 at one go. In Grace's imagination, pushing her luck that one extra mile was the only effective weapon she could use against her jealous friend Precious and Joseph's boss.

For her, it was absolutely crucial to party in Vegas as much as possible and accumulate hundreds of selfies in order to show off when she returned home.

On their final night, while they were wrapping up another romantic memory and preparing for the early morning flight back home, tragedy struck. Grace insisted one more time that they must go out for dinner and Joseph agreed. After dinner, the couple decided to quietly walk from one street to another while holding hands and taking pictures of the skyscrapers.

Shockingly, at about 10 p.m. when it was getting dark, the couple attracted the attention of three masked men. Without warning they were robbed at gun point. During the scuffle with the armed robbers Joseph was stabbed in the chest and Grace yelled for help. In a matter of minutes, the local police arrived on the scene to investigate. The police immediately called an ambulance to rush the bleeding Joseph to hospital; he was very badly injured, but at the same time stable.

At hospital he was rushed to the operating table. A female officer comforted Grace, held her hand and helped her to sit down. Due to shock and stress at that stage, Grace was crying heavily. The officer tried her best to console Grace, but to no avail.

"Young lady, I know you are extremely upset, and I can understand that, but please can you explain what happen so that we might find the criminals immediately and bring them to justice?"

Grace was completely shattered and struggled to utter even a single word, but nevertheless, the officer kept pressing her for information and she continued..

"Lady, calm down, please. Can you give me a brief description of the perpetrators and I will pass that information to my colleagues outside so that they may able to trace the criminals quickly?"

Slowly but surely, the female officer eventually managed to calm the grieving Grace down and offered her some water to drink. Grace took a few sips from the cup and then in a shaky voice she requested a tissue in order to wipe the tears raining down her cheeks. She folded her hands tight across her chest and shivering, she asked "Is he alright?"

"Oh yes, he'll be fine," the officer replied. "I am sure he is going to make it. Don't worry, just relax and tell me what happened."

"Um, I am not sure where to start. The whole episode was very quick. All that I remember is that I got grabbed from behind and I felt sharp metal on my throat. A short man violently pulled my head towards him. In broken English he yelled 'Give me your bag, give me your watch. Drop the camera on the floor and give me everything, otherwise I will kill you. I have a gun.' I was really scared; I thought he was going to kill me. Certainly he had a weapon on him, however I am not sure about what kind of weapon it was. I gave him everything that I have.

After I got myself free, I realised that Joseph was on the floor. He was lying on his stomach and they were kicking him like a football and when he tried to defend himself, then he got stabbed in the chest and they ran off with all our belongings. I panicked and I thought he was going to die. When I saw blood running from his chest, I started to scream, then people passing by came to our aid and they called you. That is all I remember."

The officer then asked "How many guys were there, and can you describe how they looked?"

"Well I am not definitely sure how they looked, because it was quite dark and they ware masked. I don't remember seeing anything useful. But they spoke broken English. Again I am not sure how many people there were. Maybe four or five. I think they were riding motorbikes." Grace concluded, and then again broke down in tears.

The atmosphere in the hospital was very tense for Grace. She feared the worst for her husband A few hours later, a surgeon doctor emerged from the operating room and he broke the good news to her that Joseph was okay.

"He is incredibly lucky to survive, though he lost a lot of blood. The knife missed his heart by just few inches otherwise it could have been fatal."

Hearing the good news, Grace took a deep breath and asked to see Joseph immediately. A doctor escorted her to intensive care. The wounded Joseph was wrapped in white blankets, flat on his back, eyes closed, and it appeared as if he was sleeping and breathing normally. Grace sat on the edge of his bed and she slightly squeezed his fingers just to reassure herself that he was still alive.

"Thank you for saving my husband's life." she told the doctor. And a moment later she went sleep lying next to him.

As dawn broke, Joseph made two loud sneezes and it woke Grace from her deep sleep.

"Joseph, how are you? Are you OK? It's me, Grace."

"I'm OK."

"Oh, thank God." she whispered.

She managed to exchange a few words with Joseph and they had a nice little conversation before a doctor came in the room and informed them that since the crime committed had involved stabbing, by Nevada law, the case would be considered as attempted murder.

"The police have informed the British consulate general about the incident, who are willing to offer consular assistance if it's necessary. It is inevitable, however, that the news will soon reach UK soil and Joseph's family will be contacted by the relevant authorities."

Grace was visibly upset and angry about that. All along she was hoping to conceal the incident from everyone, particularly Joseph's boss and her own best friend Precious. As a result, she had a heated argument with the doctor. Why would they inform the consulate general without her consent? She demanded that Joseph's family should not find out anything until they returned home, because Joseph's mother Merry was a heart patient. Grace feared that hearing such bad news may adversely affect Merry's health: in fact, it might kill her.

However, the doctor insisted that no matter what, they had to follow procedure, even if in reality the circumstances may not be favourable. To add salt to her wound, the doctor made it clear that Joseph would have to remain in the hospital for at least three weeks so that he could be fit for a long haul flight back to Britain. With extreme shock, Grace stared at him like a zombie without uttering a single word until the doctor left the room.

There is a common myth that "whatever happens in Vegas stays in Vegas" but what happened in Vegas would follow Grace and Joseph to the grave.

Two men entered in the room and tried to engage her in conversation in order to determine exactly what happened but the moment she learnt that they were reporters working for the local newspaper, she did not want to co-operate and had them thrown out.

A plain clothes officer arrived at the hospital and he asked Grace to leave the room so that he could have a little chat with Joseph alone but she refused to leave. In the absence of rationality, she attracted attention without realising it, because her odd behaviour began to somehow cast doubt on the theory of armed robbery. The officer thought that Grace might be hiding something sinister. Eventually, she was invited for questioning at the police station. During the interrogation, her demeanour was changing, however she stuck to her guns and maintained the same watertight story, yet occasionally she was extremely nervous and evasive.

The case against her was really weak. There was no eye witness except a homeless man who was sleeping rough beside the road not far from the scene. It was possible that police would charge her with the attempted murder of her husband. Without her knowledge they had tried to once again speak to Joseph at his hospital bed but unfortunately due to extreme pain, he was unable to concentrate during the interview. He was under the influence of pain killers, changed his story several times, and subsequently, Joseph was deemed not reliable. However, Grace spent a night in a cell while the police continue to build their case.

The next day, a local newspaper published the story, together with a picture of Grace and Joseph on its front page and it read:

A British tourist was robbed and received stab wounds in the chest. His wife is the prime suspect for the heinous crime.

The following day, the papers in Britain carried the same headlines. Grace's friends Fiona, Dorisa and Precious read the story: they were truly devastated and Precious broke down in tears. Immediately she left work and went straight to Grace's mother Karen in order to find out exactly what went wrong in Las Vegas. Sadly at that stage neither Karen nor Joseph's family had any information. Like Precious, everyone continued to wait in limbo.

A few days later, police granted a conditional bail to Grace and she went to the hospital to continue nursing her sick husband. The police in Vegas continue to look for evidence against the UK drama queen in the murder of her childhood sweetheart.

But a miracle was about to happen, as the faithful often predict; God can move in mysterious ways and such a prophecy was about to become reality for Grace. An old lady gave the police a promising lead after she encountered the story in the news article which had ignited her suspicious concerning a man called Carlos. This was her statement:

A day after the robbery, I was watching the morning show on TV when Carlos rushed into my room carrying several expensive items. Carlos is one of my tenants from Guatemala. Among the items he brought was a brand new designer handbag and he asked me if I was interested in buying it. I asked him where he got it from. He was very evasive in his answer. Reluctantly, he said that it belonged to his ex-girlfriend and he was selling her stuff because she no longer lived with him. He sounded nervous, and I told him that I was not interested. The description which I read in the newspaper matched the items which Carlos had.

Without hesitation, the police went straight after him and he was arrested. Handcuffed, he was interrogated at the station, where he confessed and revealed everything. Here is his statement:

Junior and I and two other friends planned to rob the couple on the night when they won $20,000 but we lost sight of them after they jumped into a taxi. We couldn't believe our luck when Junior's girlfriend spotted them again for a second time when they were having a dinner at a restaurant close to a gas station where she worked. She contacted Junior, who then called me and two other guys. That night we followed them at a distance and when it started to get dark we robbed them. I swear, we didn't want to harm them, we just wanted their money and valuables.

During the robbery, when the guy started to fight back, it was Junior who got pissed and he stabbed the guy in the chest, then we ran off. He was bleeding severely and we thought that he wouldn't make it. We panicked and Junior tried to get rid of all the evidence before him and the two other guys left for Miami. I decided to stay behind because I haven't done anything wrong. I swear on my life it was Junior who stabbed the guy in the chest. After the incident I felt awful! I am truly sorry for my participation.

Subsequently, Grace and Joseph managed to identify Carlos by his broken English and distinct voice. The police then matched his statement to Grace's version of events, and eventually, Carlos was put on trial. He was convicted for armed robbery and attempted murder and he got thrown in jail for fifteen years. Junior, a career criminal, with two other accomplices whom were all known to police are still at large and Grace and Joseph would live with the scars from the robbery for the rest of their lives.

***

Joseph's father Vladimir travelled to Las Vegas to give much needed support to his son during Carlos' trial and directed his resentment towards Grace and her family. Throughout the trial he struggled to hide his contempt for them. In his opinion, Grace was responsible for all that happened to his son and he was not alone in the view that her taste for an extravagant lifestyle had reduced Joseph from a caring son to a party animal and from a hard-working salesman to a mere servant of his stupid wife.

Her family always protested her innocence while others, including one of her co-workers, thought otherwise. In their opinion, Grace's primary concern was purely her desire to preserve the family image and save Joseph's reputation, but aroused suspicion due to her strange behaviour.

A month after the fiasco, when they were all due to return home, Vladimir refused to accompany the couple, and flew back home independently. On their return, he suggested that Grace should move out of the house and go back to her family until all the dust settled. Joseph lashed out at him and dismissed such an obnoxious suggestion as ridiculous. He yelled at his father. "Grace is my dear wife and she is here to stay and that will never change!" His remarks ignited a fire between Grace and Vladimir.

Joseph's ailing mother Merry was baffled by Grace's lack of remorse for Joseph and his family. She noticed that Grace's grief was mainly centred around the theft of her possessions and how the good memories stored in their imagination had been shattered by the robbery. Bizarrely, she kept talking about how much she missed the hundreds of pictures which they took while in Las Vegas. Merry didn't agree with her husband about Grace's potential involvement in the robbery but she was concerned for the couple's future, and encouraged Karen to provide counselling to Grace.

Surprisingly, Grace's best friend Precious, whom Grace slammed down the phone on many times and wouldn't speak to her for weeks, constantly insisted that Grace was as innocent as a new born baby and she even organized a press conference on Grace's behalf. During the entire period she was relentlessly adamant that Grace wouldn't stand to gain anything from the potential demise of her husband, and she challenged those with awful theories to come forward and produce evidence or provide a motive which would indicate otherwise. She gave interviews in order to make it abundantly clear that her friend was innocent. On their arrival she went the airport and gave them a lift home, but despite all this, the stubborn Grace continued to think Precious was jealous of her.

A few weeks later, it looked like the family was out of the woods now that Joseph and Grace had both gone back to work. It appeared that the young couple had learnt an expensive lesson in Vegas.

Nevertheless, Vladimir kept an eye on them. On one crazy Tuesday afternoon, around 1 p.m. while Vladimir was relaxing at home and thinking about taking his dog for a walk, a postman arrived with a special delivery package for Joseph. As usual, he kindly received the package on Joseph's behalf without hesitation. Out of curiosity, Vladimir decided to open it and have a look and he couldn't believe what he found. Two return air tickets to Dubai for Joseph and Grace!

As you are aware, old habits die hard. Once again the young couple were in party mode. In a few days time, it seemed they would go crazy once more and spoil each other in Dubai for two weeks.

Vladimir shook and trembled like an earthquake and he fell to the floor and screamed for help. Immediately, a neighbour ran to his aid and called an ambulance. He was rushed to hospital but after receiving a thorough check up from a doctor he was discharged the same day. A confrontation with Joseph and Grace was imminent.

Shortly after 6 p.m. he went upstairs and locked himself in his room, hoping that Joseph would check on him when he came home from work, so that he might interrogate Joseph quietly without the knowledge of his wife. But unfortunately for some reason, Joseph was late coming home. After midnight Grace arrived with Merry, who had been out for a day with her friends. Vladimir assumed that it was Joseph in the living room and ran downstairs to confront him, but instead met Grace and Merry.

He angrily asked Grace "Where is he?"

Not wanting to play ball, she shouted back "Who is 'he'?"

"The idiot!" he yelled.

"Who is the idiot?" she asked.

"Joseph!" he replied. His harshness stunned Grace and she threw the shopping bags on the sofa and went straight to her room. Merry was extremely upset and troubled by her husband's frantic behaviour and she started a heated argument with him. He tried to calm her down but failed. He attempted to go through the sequence of event which took place earlier, including his own health problems, in order to justify his actions but she wouldn't listen to him. They exchanged several nasty words until Joseph arrived at around 1 a.m.

"Mum, Dad, why are you still awake?"

Vladimir threw the airline tickets at him and slapped Joseph in the face.

"Idiot, it is you that we are arguing about! You are such a horrible useless son. Why are you taking that gold digger to Dubai? For God's sake, didn't you learn anything in Vegas?"

Joseph screamed back at him. "Come on, dad! A friend of mine lent me money for the trip. I don't care whether you like it or not, I love my wife and I will do anything to please her. Grow up, dad!"

Vladimir jumped on Joseph like a hungry lion and they started pushing and pulling each other like children fighting in the playground until Grace and Merry managed to separate them. On hearing the loud noise from next door, the neighbour who had come to Vladimir's aid earlier in the day rushed in again to find out what was going on. Eventually, she revealed the events of that Tuesday afternoon, including the emergency trip to hospital. Joseph and Merry were devastated when they learn that the old man nearly lost his life and he was extremely lucky to have survived.

***

Against all odds, a week after the fight, Joseph and his beauty queen flew to Dubai for two weeks as planned, and they left the old man behind, steaming and plotting. Merry was concerned about their extravagant lifestyle but convinced her husband to use a more gentle approach towards Joseph and Grace, but on their return from Dubai they were greeted by a letter from Vladimir and it read:

Dear Joseph,

I am not only disappointed in you but I am also angry. I regret the contract of marriage between you and my best friend's daughter Grace, whom I initially thought kind and humble, but she is selfish and deceitful. My son, you used to be obedient to me and your mother but that is no longer the case. My son, you married a woman whom I now consider to be evil and she is not only controlling all your income but also every decision that you make. Instead of being a leader, you are now a follower, and you stopped worshipping our God because you have a new one called Grace. My son, I can say for certain that Grace has taken the place of your dear mother and revered father. And she has become the caring brother as well as the passionate sister. Apart from her, nothing else matters in your life.

And my son, any man who lets his wife destroy his ego is doomed to fail in every respect. Consequently, there will be no pride left in him. My son, your lack of competence as a husband has genuinely helped Grace to destroy every trait which I and my ancestors were always known for. She has brought shame and grief to your elderly mother. My son, she not only encourages you to waste your money but also to party until late every weekend. Your attitude has completely ruined our community cohesion. As a result, our neighbours who have never complained for thirty years are now complaining about the loud music and unpleasant noises coming from our house.

My son, remember that any man who blindly follows his wife will die miserable and lonely. Any woman who takes her husband from his family is a woman who will bring shame and destruction on to him. Any parent who never plans the future for his children is the parent whose offspring dies poor. Any husband who disconnects his wife from her family is the husband who is a serial killer. Any person who fails to listen to his friends is the person who misled by others. And any man who became rich and failed to learn why his parents were poor is the man who ends in bankruptcy.

My son, it is never too late to do the right thing; be the husband and allow Grace be the wife. Instead, Grace is the husband and you are the wife. Would you prefer being a role model for society or bad example for children? My son, I might not live long enough to witness the fulfilment of my prophecy! But if you fail to take my advice you will regret why you were born.

Good luck.

Your father.

Despite this, Joseph defiantly continued to ignore his father's concerns. He even failed to acknowledge the receipt of the letter. First he hid the letter from Grace, but later he showed it to her and she read it. She felt awful and guilty. And from that moment, Grace knew that it was just matter of time before they were thrown out of the house. She suggested to Joseph that there was an urgent need to consult someone who could act as emissary between him and his father. Out of desperation she couldn't think anyone other than the former friend whom she perceived as an enemy.

Though they hadn't met for a long while, nevertheless, Grace hastily organised a dinner with Precious in order to seek her advice. At first, Precious was extremely reluctant to honour the invitation; however, when she did, she was apprehensive and cautious. She wondered why she had suddenly become important to Grace again.

They went to dinner the following night. At the dinner table, Grace sat next to her husband and Precious sat opposite. The conversation started.

"How are you, Precious?"

"I am fine," she replied.

"Look, I missed you, Precious. I am truly sorry if I ever offended you! It was a misunderstanding between us and I really feel bad about it. I realised that my behaviour in the past was pretty appalling but I hope that you will forgive me. Thanks for coming. I know I can count on you because you have always been there for me."

"Don't be silly! What are you talking about, Grace? We are friends and we will always stay friends no matter what." They both giggled shyly.

"I heard that recently you have been to Dubai for two weeks. How was your journey and how is Dubai?" She asked.

"Um, Dubai is not too bad, though it does not match Rome or Paris in terms of romance and food, I guess. It could be much better. However, I have to admit we really enjoyed our stay there, especially sunbathing on the beaches, camel riding, the bus tour, a safari in the desert, horse riding and so on. But the odd things are that we were not allowed to show affection in certain places and our friends can't even drink alcohol in public. But overall it was kind of okay."

"How about night life? Are there any clubs or pubs?"

"Oh yes. there are quite few clubs in the business district but the good ones are usually 'members only'. I fell in love with the shopping malls, skyscrapers and the gold market. I bet you our next trip will be clubbing and dining in LA."

"Wow, I wish I was lucky as you are!"

Grace laughed.

The atmosphere in the crowded restaurant was like a school reunion for Grace and Precious. When Joseph went to use the bathroom and the waiters were busy preparing to bring in the dinner, Grace whispered to her friend.

"I need your help. Joseph and his dad are at each other's throats because of me."

"Are you kidding, Grace?"

"No. I am serious. I bet you anything, by this time next week, we will be homeless. It's just matter of time before he kicks us out of the house. Here is the proof." Grace gave the letter to Precious. "Be careful, it sounds like the Ten Commandments," she joked.

Precious grabbed the letter and read it. Puzzled but not entirely surprised, quickly she gave it back to Grace.

"Oh my God, didn't you see this coming?" she exclaimed. "I told you but you wouldn't listen and you thought I was jealous of you."

They looked at each other without uttering a single word for a little while.

But Precious promised to catch up and brainstorm a solution with Grace the very next day. Joseph returned and the conversation moved on, and the delicious dinner was served. After dinner, Grace and Joseph thanked Precious and they wished each other good night.

Though she was very reliable and could keep a secret, on this occasion, Precious couldn't resist the temptation to share her thoughts with someone. Once at home, she confided with her mother what Grace and Joseph were going through. Her mother realised that Precious was genuinely concerned about her friend's well-being and suggested that Joseph should seek advice from someone within the family and then appoint an intermediary between him and his dad, perhaps a senior person like his uncle. Precious thanked her and promised to keep her mother updated.

Grace and Precious met the next day as planned. Precious noticed that her friend's appearance was really odd. She came without wearing her makeup which was very unusual. Additionally, she looked visibly saddened and sounded depressed. First, Precious tried comforting her and she cracked a few jokes in order to cheer Grace up. Then Precious said "Maya Angelou once said 'people might forget what you did for them but they will never forget how you made them feel'. Grace, I remember nine years ago when I lost my younger sister I had nightmares for three consecutive nights and when you found that out, you came to stay with us for a few days just to give me comfort. I will never forget that. My family appreciate that a lot. My mum still reminds me about it today.

I can assure you that as long as I am living, the more you run away from me, the more I will run after you! The symbol of genuine friendship is not about cheap compliments but sharing our ups and downs. Despite our past grievances, we are like soul mates. I know you have some reservations towards me and keep on telling people that I am a jealous person and never give you any compliments but that is not accurate. Grace, I am truly a sincere friend, which you deserve.

You have many ambitions, Grace, and I have many aspirations too. But don't you realise that the more ambitious you are, the less inspirational you become? Ambitious people usually like to accumulate wealth and glory and eventually they become selfish. Yet people with aspirations often grow internally, as well as helping others to grow and become even greater than their own environment. I understand that women in modern society would prefer to have equal opportunities with men.

However, it's quite common that they would expect their sons to be the protectors of their daughters. Women grow hair everywhere in their body, as men do, but biologically women cannot grow a beard because it's a symbol of leadership dictated by nature. I would suggest that you should help your husband in order for him to be like the man whom you would prefer for your daughter. Furthermore, you must be like the wife whom you would prefer for your son."

But Grace was compulsive and jumpy. She struggled to control her emotions, and she interrupted Precious.

"Excuse me, madam! I don't hate you, but I can't stand what you are talking about! I know all along that you have been confident in your opinions and I respect that. But let me be honest with you, before I consulted you, I sought advice from four close friends. Every single one of them thinks that my father in law is an idiot. I hate that ugly fat guy. He is annoying and old fashioned. He keeps on moaning about why I don't cook for his family, why I don't mop the floor and why I don't wash his clothes every weekend. This man is sick in the head. I told him so many times that I am working a full time job and I can't tolerate such a lifestyle. You have no idea. He is driving us crazy. I will never live like a traditional wife, I expect to achieve much more than that. I've had enough."

"Um, I am not sure what to tell you, but I will recommend that you stop wasting your money on luxury goods. Basically you ought to plan for the future. I kind of agree with people who believe that travelling expands your horizons, but I am afraid it won't expand yours because you are only doing it for pleasure-seeking and to show off. You cannot afford to keep wasting your money on designer clothes and gambling: it will ruin you. Pretty soon you are going to have to start to pay rent, if you know what I mean? If I was in your shoes, I would probably consider it's time now to talk to Joseph's uncle and solicit his advice for a peaceful resolution with his father. But it is up to you. Just think about it and anything you decide, please let me know. Bye bye." Precious walked away.

Grace yelled after her. "I hope you are not angry with me, Precious! So you think I should involve Joseph's uncle?"

"Of course, why not? He is more experienced than all of us." Precious called back.

"Okay, bye. See you soon. Thanks for coming!"

The following evening, Grace dragged Joseph to meet his uncle. Unfortunately for them, the uncle was not in the mood for playing teenage games, and wanted to teach Joseph a lesson which he would never forget.

"Joseph; are you good at maths?"

"Yes I am, uncle."

"Right, six minus twelve. How much left?"

"Six," said Joseph.

"Fantastic, but do you know what I'm talking about?"

"No, I don't, uncle."

"You have six months to make a baby!"

Grace shouted at him. "I am not a baby factory! We are not interested! Besides that, we cannot afford to have any children right now!"

Then uncle shouted back at her "But you can afford to get robbed in Las Vegas?"

"That's an outrageous remark, uncle. Don't make fun of our tragedy! I am quite pissed off with you. You are behaving like my dad." Joseph complained.

"Stop being silly, Joseph. You're not stupid, but you're not thinking. I will say it again: when do you guys plan to make a baby? And is she pregnant yet? Yes or no? How many times do we have to keep emphasising that in our culture, you should start a family before your first anniversary?"

"Uncle, we want travel the world in order to experience life. We don't have the mindset that you have! Your generation and ours is different. We think and plan ahead. As a young couple, we ought to enjoy ourselves as much as possible. Your culture is all about adherence to backward thinking which is why your community has failed to thrive. We are living in a modern era and we desire to live like Europeans. Our concept is totally different to yours; we believed in democracy, human rights, and the rule of law, which is all about self reliance and freedom of expression."

"Joseph, I need no lectures from you! If you desire to live like a European, go and live like one. But your attitude is in quite a contrast to Europeans! They wouldn't get married and then expect everything for free from their parents. Rent free, food free, and no bills to pay - don't try to fool me, nephew! I lived in this country for over forty years. In fact, family values are the primary concern for all Europeans. Here is my evidence: just few weeks ago, I was jogging in the park and I met a white lady who was using a walking stick. She approached me, then we had a little conversation. Guess what she said? 'I wish I could have a chance to see my children for coffee at least once every week. I missed days when we used to come together as one family and have our dinner at the table. Sadly now days it's all about money and luxury. People are workaholic. I will be lucky if I see my children once a month. I hope I will be lucky to have grand children before I die' and then she burst into tears!

Furthermore, one of my Indian neighbours living down the road owned a factory for many years. As a delivery driver, I worked for him for three years. Unfortunately, his business collapsed and as a result the family encountered many financial troubles. Eventually the bank repossessed their house and subsequently he divorced his wife with whom he had six children; four sons and two daughters. However, they weren't evicted from the property. Somehow they managed to convince the new landlord that he should allow the family to continue occupying the property as tenants until the man could marry off all his children. The landlord agreed and he renews their tenancy contract every two years. Can you imagine; each month they have to pay £2,500 as rent. The family are doing that just to preserve their reputation. In Indian culture, children find it harder to get married if their parents are separated or divorced. In their view, divorce is responsible for creating dysfunctional families.

Finally, a friend of mine from Jamaica has recently complained to me that the behaviour of her children is appalling! She said that it is embarrassing nowadays, it's all about drugs, women, drinking, smoking, swearing and getting crazy. My children insult each other in my presence. Kids no longer have respect for their parents any more. In the olden days I wouldn't dare swear or insult anyone in the presence of my parents. In those days we had the culture of discipline but that is a thing of the past. I reckon everybody wants to live like animals with no manners, and that is disgusting!

Joseph, we hold no grudge against you! But we cannot afford to risk our reputation just to please you and your Grace. I beg you please to have some mercy for your parents! Your father is a noble man and your mother is a pious lady. As a family we are extremely frustrated with your new habits. You are flying like birds, drinking like fish, and shopping like a millionaire. Don't you have any concerns about your future? You keep complaining that your dad is old fashioned but frankly he is not! Instead, it is the other way around. I can't understand how come you still fail to accommodate the idea that family reproduction is a universal concept, no matter your race, black, brown, yellow or white, basically every single family adheres to its traditions and values. That is dictated by the divine revelation which is the foundation of our social fabric."

By the time his uncle had finished talking, Joseph felt numbed and speechless. His proud demeanour was brutally crushed to anxiety. And he was visibly shaking as if he was ruptured by wild thunder. Equally, Grace's shoulders shrank as if she has been struck by lightning. Tears ran down their cheeks.

Joseph's uncle had the impression that the mighty Grace had been completely subdued, like a wounded lion. The couple did not move, for quite some time. A few moments later Grace asked for some water for Joseph, and gave it to him. She shook her head for a while then she looked at him.

"Darling, have some water, please?"

Gently she patted him on the back and she gave him a kiss.

"Don't worry, honey, we will be fine."

Grace knew precisely what she would do next. There is no doubt that Joseph's uncle's remarks lethally injected their marriage and it was now on life support. She was aware of that. It was a race against time for Grace.. she had to act, before it was too late.

2

Joseph and Grace went home late that night, feeling guilty but not entirely defeated. Shockingly, it was time for Joseph to bring up all that had been stuck inside him for a long while. Grace twice tried to give him coffee, but he refused to drink it. Outraged by his sudden awkward behaviour towards her, she asked him "What is wrong with you, Joseph?"

He shouted back "Don't shout at me, Grace! I am not a child any more! Look, we need to talk. My uncle is my strength and my father is my role model: these two guys are down to earth people. Often when I feel low, they lift my mood up. My uncle would even lend me money when am broke. My dad is always there for me and you know that.

My uncle is the most generous person in my mother's entire family. But the way he talked to me today.. he never speaks to me like that, Grace. There is no doubt that my family is genuinely concerned about our marriage and I have ignored them for so long. I think it's the time to get real. Grace, you know that I love you so dearly but in reality I wouldn't sacrifice my family just for your sake and for worldly pleasures. Today I realised that our behaviour is causing a lot of stress to so many people.. not only mum and dad, but everyone in the family. I don't want to hurt them any more.

And if you don't mind, Grace, can I ask you some important questions please?"

"Yes, go on, Joseph."

"Why don't you get pregnant? Do you take contraception, Grace?"

"Oh my God, what are you talking about, Joseph? I can't believe that you are such a horrible person! How dare you ask me a stupid question like that? What do you mean, "take contraception"? You are inadequate and you cannot even get a woman pregnant for six months and now you are trying to put all the blame on me, and for what?! You must feel ashamed of yourself, Joseph. Besides that, you told me in Paris and you also told me in Dubai that you are not interested in having any children in the next five years, but now that your horrible family is putting pressure on you, you are accusing me of taking contraception? I am really disappointed with you, Joseph."

She pushed him out of the way, left the room slamming the door behind her and went straight to her mother's house.

There, Grace got an even bigger surprise. Karen told her an excruciating story.

"Someone is using black magic on you and your husband. Just out of curiosity, last month I saw advertisement in a horoscope magazine concerning an African Voodoo Prince living in Wolverhampton, and I decided to gave him a call. The next day I went see him and here is what he told me:

someone in Joseph's family, maybe his mum or dad, is using the power of black magic on you in order to destroy your marriage! They are absolutely jealous of you and your husband's happiness," Karen exclaimed. "According to him, you will get pregnant very soon and it will be a boy, but he fears that soon after you give birth, someone will die. And guess what else he says? Joseph is about to lose his job and someone very close to him will eventually commit suicide!"

"Mum, you talk rubbish!" Grace yelled. "I don't believe in stuff like that. He is lying to you. They are just making money through deception and why do you keep wasting your money on superstition? Mum, grow up!"

"No, he is not lying, Grace, please listen to me! This guy is very powerful and famous! His readings are quite accurate! Look, what Joseph is saying to you is not normal. I am convinced that he is under the influence of a spell. Don't you realise that his behaviour is quite out of character, Grace!"

"Mum, you're so annoying! His dubious attitudes have nothing to do with spells. We have hypocrites in the family who are stirring up trouble for me and Joseph. They want break up our marriage because they adhered to the backward notion of child reproduction within one year, and as a result, Joseph and I are put under enormous pressure to follow their instructions, but over my dead body! I won't bow down to anyone. Tonight we met Joseph's uncle, who was going on and on about the importance of having a baby, but I told him loud and clear

35

that I am not interested in a family right now. My first priority is my career and making enough money to experience the world."

Grace and Karen continued arguing until early dawn and each accused the other of being stupid.

Karen, with profound agony, stubbornly continued to stick to her guns and she was adamant that Grace should use witchcraft in order to reverse the negative effect of the black magic which she believed was ruining her daughter's marriage.

She tried to take Grace to visit the Voodoo Prince, but when her attempt failed, instead of giving up on the whole idea, she invited the Voodoo Prince from Wolverhampton to confront Grace with evidence, without realising that it would take much more than this to convince the sceptical Grace. He brought along with him a few magic potions, holy water and two amulets with the intention to diagnose Grace with her symptoms of black magic but again she refused to accept the rules. The Prince and Karen were angry and upset with what they saw as obnoxious behaviour, and he left.

Grace then dropped a bombshell.

"Mum, listen to me carefully. I am warning you for the last time. You have to change your habits of superstition and spirituality, otherwise in the future, if I become a mother, I will never allow my children to stay with you! I wondered how my dad used to cope with you when he was alive. It is possible that your irritating behaviour might have actually contributed to his deterioration and death from diabetes. You act as if you are insane."

"I swear on my life, you will live to regret your action, Grace. You think you are clever, but let me tell you this: miracles do happen. Just a few months ago when you were detained in Las Vegas, I consulted a tarot card reader and he prescribed some charities which I gave out on your behalf. Barely a few hours later you, were released from police custody.

Yet you are not grateful for that, in fact when people thought that you had played a role in the Vegas robbery, again I sought prayer on your behalf from many churches and mosque across the city until all charges were finally dropped against you. How come all of a sudden you became aggressive toward me and my spirituality?"

"Mum, I was innocent! My acquittal in the court was due to the efforts of a good lawyer. It had nothing to do with the useless voodoo Prince or your charity handout!"

"Grace, listen to this sermon. 'Once upon a time, a destitute person was begging from house to house and when he reached a certain house, the occupant of the property immediately chased him away without giving him charity. Then many years later, that person divorced his wife and she got married again to another man. While she was with him, a beggar knocked at the door looking for help and he was chased away like before. However, on this occasion the wife burst into tears; and she said to her husband: do you know who was begging? No I don't, the husband responded. It was my ex-husband, she exclaimed.

He was extremely wealthy and powerful before, but now he is poor and destitute. I remembered once upon a time while I was married to him he did exactly the same as you did today! A beggar came to the door and he was chased away by my ex-husband without giving him the charity. The new husband said, that beggar was me. I am rich now and your ex-husband is poor.'

Additionally, a wise man said 'A fish and a little bird fell in love and they desired to live together as couple. But where would we live? the fish asked. The little bird suggested that a crocodile must be consulted for ideas as to how they could survive in the sea and the shore. The fish asked the crocodile and she agreed to share ideas but with two conditions. The crocodile wanted to learn from the fish how to lie for ages in the water and be safe. The crocodile warned the fish not to approach the shore without first getting permission from her to ensure that there are no dangers waiting for her. A few moments later the fish changed her mind. She thought that teaching the crocodile with such vital information would be a catastrophic mistake and she broke the agreement without informing the crocodile. Days later, she went out wandering and looking for her lover, the little bird. She was caught by a fisherman, and the little bird then went and married the crocodile and they lived together happy ever after. Therefore, Grace, don't be like the ex-husband and become poor and destitute, or the fish, a betrayer and then fall on your own sword."

"Wow, mum, that was a very fascinating story! It could mesmerise someone and capture their imagination, but here is my story. At the secondary school library, I read a powerful snippet in a book. It was outstanding. In the late forties at Manchester city there were two friends working in a clothes factory. Every week, one friend would donate at least £10 to charity and the other would spend £10 buying new books. And twenty years later, the generous friend has donated well over £10,000 and the curious friend had read well over 1,000 books and eventually he went and published his own ground-breaking story book. Thus, amazingly he won the Nobel Prize for literature. Then many years later, the generous friend died but sadly he had no money left for the funeral because he had donated everything to charity. His curious friend paid off all his debts and arranged his funeral.

A few weeks after the funeral, the Imam had a vision. In his vision he saw the two friends entering the paradise together, holding each other's hand and they were wandering from one garden to the other surrounded by the beautiful flowers.

Mum, from this illustration, I will encourage you to carry on giving out charity and I will continue accumulating wealth, in case one day you become poor, then I will look after you. If I fail to make it to paradise, you can rescue me wherever I am and take me there. Mum, your psyche and mine are quite different. We desire not to learn the past from the clairvoyant, but from a museum. Equally we learn the present not from the psychic and the medium, but in schools and universities. Finally, we love to learn the future not by tarot card readers, astrologers and fortune tellers but by doing research and reading books. Mum, my message to young people is clear: if you want know the past, visit the museum. If you want know the present, enrol at school, and if you want know the future, get yourself a library card."

3

After the terrible argument with Grace, Joseph was at his wit's end. He didn't know whether to call her, or if she would even listen to him. He kept looking at his phone, hoping that it would ring and Grace would be on the line, but he had no idea what he would say.

The only thing he could think of was that it might be useful to learn about relationships from other people, and get their opinions. A guy from Pakistan called Shakour was Joseph's co-worker. He was physically attractive, but he hardly socialised with anyone. Out of curiosity, Joseph asked him "Shakour, how did you meet your wife?"

"I woke up one morning and looked in the mirror for a while and I wondered why I was still single. In the past few years, I had dated many girls, but without success. I kept asking myself why I failed to attract women. Was it because I am clever but not very intelligent? Was I nice looking but not very kind hearted? Was I healthy but not slim enough? What was the problem and what was the solution?

I decided to attend my friend's birthday the following weekend, because I thought there would be some single women there, and I promised myself that I would strive to find a soul mate. Enough was enough. I couldn't face any more humiliations. A few days before his birthday, I went to the market and I bought some smart clothes, just to ensure that I felt special on that day, with the intention of finding someone special too. Many people planned to attend that event, including some of my own family."

Joseph interrupted him. "But what were you doing with your life for all those years?"

"I was just working, making money and looking after my parents, but now I was looking for someone to settle down with."

"Can you please tell me the key to making this happen?"

"Be content and live within your means. I like shopping and wearing nice clothes all the time but I am content. So I bought a black top and some sharp trousers and they cost me approximately £250. That's quite a lot, isn't it? But I was still living within my means!"

"So what happened next?"

"The day before my friend's birthday, I went shopping and I bought a Thom Ford aftershave to make sure that I smelled nice and felt good about myself. But my biggest challenge remained: I lacked confidence. I wanted to make sure that I did all I could to control my nerves. Before the party started, I thought everything through beforehand, and I wanted be successful like my friend Marcuse.

At the party, I went up to him and said "Hello Marcuse, how are you? I wish you a very happy birthday."

"Thanks," he said. "You look really smart, Shakour, I guess tonight will be your night. Make sure you find your soul mate!" He laughed. Though he was busy welcoming the guests and receiving gifts from them, I quickly asked him for a favour.

"What are your tips to attract women, Marcuse?"

"O my God, Shakour, what are you talking about? You are nearly thirty years old and you really don't know how to attract women? Are you kidding me?"

"I am not joking. Seriously, I don't have any experience in dating women!"

"How do you usually do it?"

"Here we go.. firstly, I buy them lot of flowers, and usually I tell them how beautiful they look. That's all. I don't say much because most of the time I am extremely nervous."

Marcuse laughed again. "Do you see that girl with the dark hair standing next to my girlfriend? Her name is Joy and she is my girlfriend's best friend. If you like the way she looks, why can't you try your luck with her?"

"You are right. She looks very beautiful. I wish she would show interest in me. I will try as you had suggested. You never know. I could be lucky."

"Here are some tips for you. Beautiful women are the most powerful creatures walking on the face of this planet, hence they can be very intimidating, but she could fall in love if you act with confidence. There are four rules which you have to follow when you approach them. 1. Don't comment on her beauty. 2. Don't follow her orders. 3.

Don't buy expensive gifts for her. 4. Don't express any sexual desires towards her until it's appropriate. If you manage to follow the rules, slowly but surely she will fall for you."

"What about if I forget the rules? What else can I do?"

"Just be yourself and follow your own rules."

"I never heard such rules before. Can you please explain to me why they are important?"

"Firstly, a beautiful woman knows that she is very beautiful, and that is exactly what other guys are telling her. However, by you not telling her that she is beautiful, she will wonder why you are not commenting on her beauty as others do. That will encourage her to get to know you more.

Don't take orders from her. If you don't, she will be thinking 'How dare you not take my orders!'. She will be curious and gravitate more towards you. If you buy her expensive gifts that is exactly what she will get from other men, and she would think that you are trying to buy her loyalty. Finally don't express any sexual desires towards her: that is exactly what she is worried about thus she might think it's is all about sex for you and nothing else. Shakour, you should understand that a women does not care how much she lost today, but she does care what she might gain in the future. That is precisely why it is important to act differently."

"Thanks for your advice, Marcuse," I said.

I approached Joy and introduced myself and she looked me straight in the eye. I was feeling confident and friendly. I gave her few compliments and I told her that I admired her blue dress, and she asked me "Is blue your favourite colour?" and I said yes. Then a few moments later I walked away and I came back again for the second time to make sure I followed the rules that Marcuse suggested.

Marcuse was curious to find out what was going on between Joy and me and I explained everything to him. He thought that Joy and I would be an item soon because Joy too was eager to settle down. Marcuse patted me on the back.

"Shakour, you are so intelligent!" said Joseph. "You seem to follow the rules and in the end you have been successful. I don't blame you because occasionally some men find it harder talking to women but eventually they would test the water and become successful. So what happened after that?"

"We danced for a while and I was acting funny just to make people laugh but honestly, we really enjoyed ourselves. The party continued until late, then everyone went home. Before Joy left, I realised she was very keen to see me again and I think the way I entertained her was very special. The next day, Marcuse told me that she was quite impressed with the way I danced. After the party I didn't hear from her for a while, but then luckily she called me and we met for a drink. On our second meeting, she asked me what kind of music I liked. And she also asked why at age 30 I was not married. I felt awful and I didn't know what to say, but to distract her I said that I liked pop music. "Do you like Italian music?" she asked? I didn't really, but I nodded. "I have lot of CDs, Indian music and Italian music." she said. I was little bit shy at the beginning but she was very talkative and she asked all sorts of questions. The following day we met again, and since then, we catch up every other day and she lends me different CDs. We didn't kiss or hug or anything for a long time, and then one day she joked "If you don't kiss me tomorrow you will have to wait for one year!"

It appeared that everything was perfect between me and her, and I continued to adhere to Marcuse's 'play book'. In the following few months we build our relationship around love and understanding. I even struggled to make time for my friends, then all of a sudden, one day someone called and said "Hello Shakour!"

"Who is that?" I said.

"It's Marcuse! You don't remember me any more because Joy is your new friend." he laughed. But I see him when I can. Often we go for lunch and I tell him about the CDs I borrow from Joy.

Then all of sudden, Joy stopped seeing me for a while. I called her one night, she said I've been very busy lately so I wasn't able to contact anyone, but stay cool, I will see you later tomorrow evening. We met as she promised and since then we've never stopped seeing each other. She thought that I was dating someone else because she felt that I was not showing enough interest in her despite our seeing each other almost every day. Two weeks later, I invited her for dinner and we spent the night together in my house for the first time."

"I am sure that as a couple, you have experienced some ups and downs. What are they?" asked Joseph.

"Well, one day we had been out for dinner and I forgot my wallet, so she had to pay for the whole dinner.. trust me, she went crazy and exploded like a firework. At the beginning, my parents were not very pleased with the idea of my marrying her because she came from a different social class to me. Nevertheless I managed to convince them and finally they gave us their blessing and we got married and we are living together happily.

Right now, our main challenge is that one of her friends called Bibi is a trouble maker. In any society there is always someone who is partying like there is no tomorrow, and Bibi is the type of woman who only see men as liabilities, not assets. She will called you honey only if you are prepared to open your wallet. She is really close to my wife. And she can be a darling to any man who is ready to part with his money. She often says I am a free spirit with little moral value. Usually when we are out, she only shows interest in older guys and people whom she thinks are vulnerable and she calls them my baby sugar daddies.

Often she has a one night stand with a man and the next day she doesn't want know them. She is constantly dreaming of becoming rich. To be fair, also there are men in society who desire to live precisely like Bibi, who use women and then turn their back on them. We've tried to straighten her out a few times but it is almost impossible to

47

achieve. However, we will continue trying. For Bibi, the symbol of success is luxury goods and fancy vehicles. We've had a massive argument about that. She can be a bad influence on my wife. Despite that, she is friendly sometimes but occasionally she can be deadlier than the devil. This type of attitude is common nowadays especially among young people. They think they can get whatever they can from a person and then dump them. I guess it's a common trend now."

Joseph agreed. "Greedy people are the worst human beings. They admire the wrong kind of people and often they act like someone they are not. If a human being lacks moral values and good judgement, they don't feel shame, or care about hurting others. Bibi is arrogant and oblivious to rational thinking. You should disconnect her from your wife, otherwise your wife will lead her life according to what she expects for herself, not what you expect of her."

Shakour said "My dad always says this; if you are living in cities and towns you should be careful of gold diggers. He or she often looked very beautiful, they dress smartly and they sound intelligent in order to impress you. They float along with anyone just to attract them but if you blindly follow such people they will take you to the cleaners.

A friend's girlfriend frequently asked him to buy this and that for her and she came up with fake stories to extract sympathy from him, like 'I was abused by my ex boyfriend, I was beaten by my ex husband, I was molested by my uncle'. In the end he found out she was lying. None of it was true. She was just making up stories in order to make money. It takes only seconds to fall in love with a manipulative person, because often he or she gives the impression that they are a victim of some sort. By the time you realise fact from fiction, they are long gone and you will live to regret it forever."

"I really appreciate your time. Thanks, Brother Shakour."

On Thursday morning, Joseph jumped from his bed to embark on a journey which he'd planned in advance to Manchester, in the north of England. It was the first time he'd been there alone. He had his usual morning shower, ate his breakfast and brushed his teeth. He was meticulous in examining his car before the journey, and was very careful in traffic on his way through the city streets to reach the motorway. He was apprehensive, and he didn't want anything to go wrong. He took regular breaks along the way, and entertained himself with the radio, which kept his emotions in check.

In his mission to find out about relationships and how they worked, he'd turned to Tinder. He'd hooked up with a woman from the north, and though he didn't really know what he was doing, or how it would help, he figured out that she was a pleasure seeker, and at least, if all went well, she might take his mind off his problems for a short while.

It was a disaster. Once in the city, he was extremely disappointed to find out that the woman was married and she was still living with her husband. His expectation of exhausting two packets of Viagra which he carried with him was thrown in the ocean. They met briefly. She apologised for dragging him up to Manchester, said what a nice boy he seemed, and kissed him on the cheek. She knew her behaviour was outrageous and a big mistake, but out of politeness she offered to pay for a hotel so that he could see the city and his journey wasn't totally wasted.

Joseph refused to accept her offer and wearily started the drive back to London. There was no reason for him to stay in the north: the only thing he'd learnt was a lesson about the fickleness of relationships.

The experience Joseph had in Manchester has re-inforced his believed that every aspect of human life is like a journey. Every journey ends at a destination but occasionally it might not be the ideal destination. If you encounter any disappointment along the road, you should learn from that and move on with your life. Perhaps some would argue that any journey which is made in order to commit a sin will always end in disappointment, but what Joseph leant from this journey was that marriage is like a vehicle which you have to prepare for a long journey. Love and understanding is the engine of that vehicle. You ought to expect challenges because there will be trial and turbulence along the way, and sometimes, out of frustration, you find more questions than answers.

To refresh himself a little, Joseph called into a cafe to get a strong coffee for the first part of his journey. He got talking to a gentleman from Africa called Musa, who was in need of a lift to the capital, and Joseph decided to help. The journey would be less boring with someone along for the ride. As they drove along together, the young man recounted an astonishing story.

According to Musa, a young couple he knew, Lamin and Isha, had been secretly dating for nearly two years, and they decided to get engaged. A few weeks later they announced that they were getting married. Lamin was a 20 year old boy, known by his nickname "L". He was handsome, dark and tall. He met Isha at high school, but they belonged to different tribes, and Lamin's family was not as religious as Isha's. Despite that, he had a huge respect for them.

Lamin's parents always encouraged him to be a good person and to study hard, especially Bintou, his mother. She told him to take his education seriously and not be a distraction in the classroom! He became one of the best students, and developed a habit of studying in the library. Sometimes he would read books for hours.

One day he noticed a pretty girl sitting by herself in a corner of the library. He wanted to approach her but he found it difficult due to social stigma. Isha was attractive. She always wore a long Muslim dress which covered almost all her body. L had a desire to marry a such a religious person. He tried to make eye contact several times but she didn't notice him.

One day at lunch time, he decided to test the water. He calmly walked toward Isha and introduced himself. Finally, for L and Isha the game had begun, and very soon the school was not only a learning place for the pair, but also a romantic one. The next day he joked to Isha "If you wish, just call me L!"

"Um, 'L', that's funny. How old are you, L?" she asked.

"I am 20. How old are you?"

"I don't know my real age. I still live with my parents."

L and Isha continued to chat until the end of their lunch time. From that day, the pair kept in touch at school and outside it. They had a strong feeling for each other and eventually they fell in love. However, due to their tribal differences, neither L nor Isha could declare the relationship to their parents. If they wanted to get married, it would be a battle.

Isha pretended to be extremely religious, and for many months she denied even a kiss to L. One afternoon he asked again, and she agreed to kiss him, but only if it was out of sight behind the school fence.

"Why behind the school fence?" L asked.

"I don't want to risk ruining my reputation. Besides that, according to religious scholars, your guardian angels and mine will relax when we are out of sight so it's the perfect place for kissing."

From then on, the secret lovers kicked off their 'behind the fence' habit until end of the school term. However, they were half-kisses in fear of discovery, because if they were caught they would be thrown out of school.

Joseph interrupted Musa's story.

"My friend, that sounds so stupid! How can someone believe in guardian angels?"

"No, its real, Joseph!" Musa exclaimed. "In religious societies, most people believe that each individual has a guardian angel watching all their actions and protecting them from harm. It's like a kind of CCTV, watching everything you do."

"Oh I understand now, to me it sounds like a deterrent to behaving badly. So what happened next?"

Musa continued his story..

Eventually, L stopped coming to school for a little while. Isha was really concerned for his well-being and she did whatever she could to find out what was happening. Luckily someone from his class knew exactly where he lived. He gave Isha directions and the next day after school she visited L. At the door, Isha was received by Bintou, who welcomed Isha but struggled to hide her intense curiosity, because Isha was the first girl to ever visit L.

Isha wasted no time and she told Bintou why she was there. Isha surprise visit really excited Bintou. She was happy Isha really cared about L, and she made her feel comfortable, as if it was her own home. She called upstairs for L, telling him that a pretty girl called Isha was waiting for him.

He jumped from his bed, quickly put on his clothes and rushed to greet Isha. They went in the hallway and they hugged and kissed in front of his mum.

"What happened to you?" Isha asked.

"I had a recurrence of malaria, which why I couldn't go to school."

"I am sorry to hear that. Without your kiss I felt lost for so many days! I felt strange and awful. I was wondering what was wrong with you, because since I know you, you have never been absent from class. I thought the worst and I decided to come and check on you. It's awesome that you sound so well and I am grateful to God that you are now recovering from malaria. May He restore your full health. I'm not sure what your mother must think of me, I should go."

"No, please don't leave, my mother is fine. Please stay for a little while. We need to talk and I really missed you so much, Isha." He kissed her again.

"Me too. You haven't a clue as to how much I missed you."

"Isha, your kiss to me is the best medicine. I feel so much better now and I think we should declare our relationship to the outside world and marry next year. What do you think?"

"Due to our tribal differences, it will be a miracle if we get married! But let's hope for the best. Just make sure you are 100% recovered by next week."

She stayed for a while, then later in the evening returned home. She gave no thought to her own parents, who where seriously wondering why she took so long to come home from school. She made her excuses, but from her mother Tida's body language, Isha knew there was soon going to be a massive problem.

While Isha expected a confrontation with her parents about her suspicious behaviour, Bintou and his father Karamba were about to encourage L to marry her. Bintou broke the news of Isha's visit at the dinner table. Karamba was delighted.

"You should have brought her home earlier! Someone might have stolen her away from you. I wouldn't mind a marriage between you and such a virtuous girl!"

They all laughed. From that moment, L knew that his parents would soon be thinking of approaching Isha's parents. He had not quite recovered from malaria, but the next day L forced himself to attend school in order to break the good news to Isha.

During the morning break he dropped the fantastic news. Isha was truly shocked and she asked L "Are you sure this is going to work?"

"I am sure 100%. But you don't look well. Why?"

"Oh really, I guess it's to do with my family."

"What happened yesterday? Did you have an argument with them?"

"I got home late and my parents were doing my head in. I told them that I was alone all day, but they struggled to digest my story, especially when I told them that I had an assignment at the school, and that is why I came home late."

"Are you ready to confront your parents about me? How will you introduce me to them? Do you really think they'll have a negative reaction?"

Isha yelled "I wouldn't dare tell my parents about you, otherwise they will kill me! Are you crazy? I told you so many times that our parents are totally different. My family are so strict."

Isha and L had no idea how to solve this problem. Eventually, he said "My mum is smart. She'll know how we can consult your parents. I am worried about my dad, though. He joked about it but he still didn't grasp the your family background is so different. What excited my mother the most was your dress, your attitude towards her and the way you look generally. My dad hasn't even met you. All he knows about you are the things mum told him. We will have to take our time!"

Becoming braver, the lovers started to go out together more often than before and a few eyebrows were raised in the neighbourhood. However, L and Isha couldn't care less about anyone else. They were engrossed in each other's company.

One evening Isha's sister, who was always looking for trouble, spotted them kissing down at the beach. She immediately alerted her parents, who started to monitor all Isha's movements. Out of sympathy for Isha, her big sister felt the need to inform her about the family surveillance. Isha was shocked to the core; and the next day, she informed L about the new developments. They became more vigilant whenever they met.

The risky lovers continued to play 'catch me if you can'. Almost every day after school they would visit each other and come home whenever they wished. L's parents broke their silence and told him that Isha's family had become suspicious about their relationship and sometime soon, something would happen.

You can see there was a huge difference in how the families behaved. Where there was a rumour, L was usually the first to know, in contrast to Isha's family who kept quiet and gathered evidence against her in order to put a stop to her relationship.

Out of frustration, Isha's family hastily planned an arranged marriage for her. Her father Muhammad would not allow any of his daughters to marry someone outside of the tribe. Previously he had forced two of Isha's sisters into endogamy against their will. Tida had secretly negotiated Isha's marriage proposal to a cousin of hers.

L planned to confront Isha's family with his own proposal for marriage. The local custom is that the oldest in the family should marry. L marrying Isha at an age of 20 would still enable him to pursue a higher education in the West to fulfil his childhood dream of becoming a doctor. But L was extremely concerned about Isha's family surveillance and Karamba sat him down many times to give him advice.

"L, do you really love Isha?"

"Yes I do, dad."

"What is your intention for her in the future?"

"I would love to marry and settle down."

"Are you willing to sacrifice your life for her if it's necessary?"

"Yes, dad. Isha means the world to me. I will sacrifice anything in the world to get her. She gave me hope and a reason to live my life."

"I hear you loud and clear, my son You have my endorsement to marry Isha. However, don't do anything stupid. Don't visit her family home just yet. Make sure that she feels safe with you all the time. And if there is any trouble from her family or from anyone else, I will be there to support you guys."

"Thank you, dad. I am very proud of you, and I promise to take your advice. Wish me luck. One day I will marry her, after my graduation."

L was confident that it was all going to be OK. Meanwhile, in Isha's home, all was quiet. However, she was relying on her big sister for information, in case any rumour concerning her relationship with L surfaced. In the following few days when she went to school, she would kept her distance from L, just to avoid a possible confrontation at home but L was not able to resist temptation for long. He tried to approach Isha many times so that he could reveal his parents approval of their relationship. Often he would be inpatient to get her attention and give her the good news, however, despite his best efforts, Isha was not giving him any chance to meet, due to fear of her parents. He wondered if their relationship was heading for a separation.

One weekend he could not wait any longer and he decided to visit Isha's home against his father's wishes. He went along quietly without anybody knowing.

Before he left the house, he dressed in a white Muslim dress as if he was going to the mosque for prayers, thinking that if they met, he might impress Muhammad, because he knew that her father was an imam.

On the way, L visited one of Isha's best friends who lived not far from him. He asked her to call Isha to make sure that she would be at home, and not to tell anyone about it. At first she was reluctant, bearing in mind how strict Isha's parents were, especially with people from outside her family. But eventually he convinced her to make the call, and they found out that Isha would be at home for the rest of that evening. L was delighted and he thanked her, and then went straight to the mosque to pray for a successful outcome. At that point he was nervous and he started to doubt himself. It was about 6 o'clock in the evening.

He went quickly to Isha's compound and he calmly walk past her father at the gate, but surprisingly on that Sunday evening Isha's extended family were visiting, chatting and laughing amongst themselves. L saw many different faces, but the thing which scared him the most was that majority of them wore strict Muslim dress. The way they all looked at him, he wondered if they thought that he was a thief or someone who was lost. He decided to quickly turn back and return home but someone yelled out "Hello, young man. Who are and you what are you looking for? How can I help you?"

He took a deep breath and then he said "I am looking for Isha." Everyone turned around to look at him, because it was out of character for a boy to come into that Sarahule compound and ask about a girl.

And a man asked him "You are looking for Isha? Who are you?"

"I am her schoolmate," L replied.

"What is your name?"

"My name is L."

"Excuse me, can you repeat your name?"

"I said my name is L!"

Then the man came closer to him and in an angry voice said "Yes, but what is your real name?"

Finally L said "My full name is Lamin."

The man then introduced himself as Isha's elder brother. Everybody was looking at L and listening to their conversation. Isha was in the kitchen, cooking dinner for her family. Her younger sister who was always jealous, came up to her and told her that someone called L was asking for her. Isha was shocked but knew it was true because nobody in her family, except her big sister, knew about L.

Shocked, Isha stood there and took deep breaths. She knew that there would be a nasty reaction from her family. At the same time she thought "How dare he do this to me? I told him not to ever come here. Oh my God, he has ruined my life."

A few moments later, her big brother angrily called her.

"Do you know this guy?!"

"Yes I do," she said, in a shaky voice. "He is my classmate."

"Didn't I tell you not to befriend boys?" He turned around to face L and said "Tell me why you are really here."

Instead, L turned his attention to Isha. "I decided to visit you today just to say hello, because on Friday at school you were not in a good mood, so that is why I decided to surprise you, just to make sure that you are alright."

But at that moment, it was clear to everyone that L was her boyfriend. All of sudden her brother grabbed Isha, slapped her, and the rest of the family joined in, swearing and calling her all sorts of names. Isha's uncle Omar started to push and pull L and threatened to kill him if he came to visit Isha again.

L tried free Isha from her brother, who let her go and started to struggle with L. L realised that he had managed to free Isha, and he broke free, ran out, jumped the fence and hurried back to town.

Isha also ran out of the compound and she disappeared into the neighbourhood. Someone in the family started to run after her but her father stopped him, and gathered everyone together in the living room. He wanted know precisely what had happened, while Isha's mother yelled that Isha had brought shame on their family. It took a while for everyone to calm down and her father began to talk to them all.

"I was extremely embarrassed and disappointed with you, my eldest son. How you could you attack your sister and her supposed boyfriend without any proof of wrong doing?"

"Dad, they are sinners! Don't give them any benefit of doubt."

Muhammad angrily stood and shouted at him. "Shut up! How dare you interrupt me while I speak? Have some manners, and get out of my sight!" Isha's brother left the room in disgrace.

Muhammad then turned around to Tida and yelled at her. "Stop crying! She will never break up our family and she will never bring shame on our family either. You should realise that young girls are like this nowadays. It's wrong to befriend a boy, but we do not know if they have done wrong. In Islam, before we jump into any conclusion or be judgemental, we need to have evidence which would prove a sin beyond any reasonable doubt. We must go and tell Isha that she is free to come home."

His approach surprised everyone. They didn't expect such tolerance from a strict father like him, but they knew deep down that is was exactly how a responsible father should behave.

L went straight round to a friend's house. He revealed his ordeal and was visibly shaking from shock and he asked his friend if he could stay with him for a few days, because he didn't really want his family to find out what had happened. His friend too was pretty shocked and angry about Isha's family's nasty reaction. He suggested to L that they must go and report the matter to the police. "This is very serious. They could have killed you!"

"Oh no." L said, "Just leave it. I will be fine. I am worried about Isha though. I don't know what she is going through right now. All this is my fault. I should not have gone there in the first place. She warned me several times that I should not visit her home. My father said that too, but I was stupid and I brought shame on everyone."

His friend calmed him down, and late into the night, they worked out what to do next.

The following day, L and Isha were absent from school. Isha's friend wondered why. After school hours on that day, she decided to call L and Isha to find out why they didn't turn up. She called Isha first, and she received the devastating news from Isha's sister of what had happened the evening before. She was thrilled, but not surprised, and immediately left her home and headed to Isha's with the intention of joining the search. Isha couldn't be found the next day, but two days later, Isha's family received a tip off that she was hiding in the house of a neighbour. Tida passed that information to Muhammad and he went and brought Isha home. He warned everyone that they should stay away from Isha and leave her alone while she recovered from the trauma.

Five days after the incident, L still had not told anything to his parents. However, Karamba, who was a trained nurse, noticed from L's body language that he was not behaving as usual and slightly limping on his left side. He decided to confront him.

"What is going on, L? Lately you are behaving very strangely."

"I am fine, dad, I am suffering from flu that is all."

"I don't believe that, L. Having the flu is no reason to stay away from home. Eventually, I will find out what is happening," he warned.

The next day Bintou found out from someone at her work place that her son had been beaten by Isha's family. She was shocked and sickening by such a revelation. When she returned home, she informed her husband. In the evening they confronted L and they forced him to tell the truth. Finally he revealed the sequence of events which took place at Isha's home six days earlier. Before he could finish, Karamba yelled at him. "I told you, idiot! Never visit her at home!"

"Dad, I wanted to prove to the whole world that I love Isha and she means the world to me! Didn't I tell you that I am willing to sacrifice my life for her if necessary and I will do anything to protect her?"

His father relented. His parents hugged him and they reassured him that everything would be okay, and Isha would be his wife one day. Bintou suggested seeking an intervention from a holy man.

"Where can we find the holy man?" L asked.

"He lives at Brikama. Let's go and meet him right now, so that you can receive his blessing," Bintou insisted, and Karamba agreed. They quickly got a taxi to Brikama.

At the holy man's residence, they found many people waiting outside, and they joined the queue, decided to see him together as one family. When it was their turn, Karamba told the holy man the reason why they were there.

The holy man looked at L for a while. Eventually he said "You will marry that girl one day, after which, you will both travel together to Europe to further your education. I can see that one day you will become a famous lawyer and the whole country will love to know you personally."

He gave them some holy water to drink, as well as to wash in for seven days. After that he said that they should kill a white sheep and then share the meat amongst seven people. He promised them that after doing that, their wishes would come true. L and his family were overwhelmed with joy and returned home hoping for a better future.

L asked Bintou "Mum, I was really mesmerised by what he said. How does he really know what has happened between us, and how does he know that I will become a lawyer?"

"He is a gifted clairvoyant, that is why he is able to predict your future."

The following day L and Isha returned to school, the first time they met after the incident. Isha arrived early, and when she saw L coming, she ran to embrace him, which surprised everyone. She jumped around and gave him a big kiss in public for the first time since they started dating, and she screamed out loud "L, you are my hero!"

L never expected such a positive reaction from Isha. All along he was wondering if it would take time for them to recover from their ordeal, and he had even hinted to a few friends that it would take time before they could even consider a reunion. He was so happy, and before lessons began, the two of them talked for a while.

Isha learned that it was her girl friend who caused the trouble in the first place. Isha was disappointed about her friend's failure to warn her in advance that L had planned to visit her. She wanted to confront her friend but L stopped her. It just wasn't worth the trouble.

Before they left the school that day Isha said to L "Be mindful and watch out for my big brother!"

"How about your dad?" L asked.

"My dad is okay for now and he promised to talk to me about us when the time is right."

Lamin the Mandinka and Isha the Sarahule continued to date for one more year. Eventually they tied the knot and migrated to the UK to further their education. Now L is a lawyer as predicted by the holy man and they are blessed with three beautiful children. Isha was the only girl in the family who was allowed to marry into a different tribe and now she is a full time nurse working in the NHS.

Joseph said to Musa "I wish my dad was as supportive as Isha's dad. The way he handled the situation was much better than how my dad treats us. But anyway, I will continue with my struggle."

4

Downcast after his Manchester experience, though grateful for meeting Musa, Joseph had to get away from it all. At least on holiday, I'll get a good rest, in nice weather, he thought. He jumped online and booked a break to the far East, to Myanmar.

On holiday, one morning, a Buddhist Monk dressed in yellow approached Joseph in the cafe while he was having breakfast. They talked for a while, and Joseph tried to tell the monk some of his story. The monk teased Joseph. "If you don't take care of your lover, perhaps someone else will and precisely that is what happened to Danjoo!"

"Who is Danjoo?" asked Joseph.

"A long time ago in our village, a coastal town we call Coco, there were no boundaries in the community. We lived together as one family and for survival we depended on farming and fishing. Every year, the villagers would organise a festival for lovers. Boys and girls would compete to dance in circles for at least an hour and then adults would join them. However, every boy in the village dreamed of being with the most beautiful girl in the town: if she liked him, then eventually she would marry him as a traditional wife. When it was Danjoo's turn to choose a wife, he picked Mami from the crowd and they danced together for a while before we all joined in. At the end of festival Danjoo and Mami started to date each other.

In our tradition we don't allow even a child to stay with women in the darkness. But Danjoo and Mami broke our rule many times. They were very stubborn. Danjoo would sneak out of his home when night fell and he would spend time with Mami until dawn. For some reason, people were not alarmed by that, in fact the villagers turned a blind eye, as if nothing was happening. They could have fun as much as they wished. Other boys really did admire them."

"How old was Danjoo?" asked Joseph.

"He was about 15 years old and Mami was roughly the same age."

"Can you describe how they looked?"

"Danjoo had a fair complexion, and was tall and skinny. Mami was a very pretty girl. I wish you could see her."

"So what happened?"

"In our tradition, every Friday, women fetch water from the sea and men gather firewood from the bush.

Usually we don't allow young boys to do this due to the dangerous reptiles, but occasionally boys would accompany the women to the sea. While women fetched the water, the boys liked to swim in the ocean and sometimes they liked showing off to girls. One day when it was Mami's turn, Mami and other girls went to the sea without any male protection protection. A strange man came from nowhere and he kidnapped Mami, threw her in his canoe and paddled off. During the commotion, one girl died on the spot of shock and the rest ran for their lives.

A boy bravely ran into the bush and he told us what had happened. Straight away, we ran to the shore, but when we arrived we couldn't see anything except wave after wave. A local fisherman noticed us, and recounted that twice that week, while fishing, he saw several strange looking men in the ocean in small canoes. They appeared to be lost and they asked him for directions to a certain village. He couldn't really work out who they were. He had never seen anyone so foreign and frightening. So we had a feeling that Mami had actually been kidnapped by a spirit. Whether you believe it or not, there are lot of spirits in the ocean!" the monk exclaimed, and then continued with his story.

"When Danjoo heard that Mami had gone, he cried and he wanted to jump into the ocean but I grabbed him and we dragged him away from there and took him home. The people in the village wept along with Danjoo. It was really heartbreaking."

"Did you inform the police about it?" asked Joseph.

"Oh no, in that village, there was no need for police, our beliefs were in magic and prayers only. Danjoo fainted on the floor and he was unconscious for almost two days. I prepared some local medicine for him and I treated him until he recovered. Danjoo's mother and father were so traumatised that I thought that they were going to die. In our culture when something like that happens, we mourn for a week without consuming food, we only drink water and fruit juice.

Mami's parents fervently believed that one day she would come back home alive: they never even shed a single tear.

We thought that due to the sudden shock that they were in denial. The senior man in the village consulted a spiritual master in the jungle, who revealed that Mami has been kidnapped by an alien king, who would steal all the beautiful girls in the towns and villages and sacrifice them in order to protect his kingdom from human interference.

The spiritual master instructed us to kill a black cow on Wednesday night and told us that we should not consume the meat. Instead, we should throw the meat in the ocean and after that we must wait on the river bank to witness what was to happen. If the crocodiles ate the meat, then within three days we would hear some good news about Mami. If they didn't, it wasn't a good sign; it would mean that Mami was no longer alive. We did exactly as he suggested.

When we placed the meat in the ocean, the villagers went home, leaving two of us at the river bank to observe what was to happen. We waited for many hours without any sign of crocodiles and then I fell asleep. Shortly before dawn, there was a big commotion in the water which woke us up but we were too frightened to look. My friend panicked and ran, then I ran after him.

In the morning, we were asked what happened and precisely we described what occurred the night before, and people were very delighted about it. Everyone genuinely thought that the commotion in the water was the crocodiles consuming the meat, but we were not sure about that. It could have been anything because we didn't stay to look and I felt guilty. But nonetheless, five days later, Danjoo has a vision about Mami in a dream.

According to the dream, Mami and three other girls were imprisoned somewhere far into the jungle on an island in the middle of the ocean. So in order to rescue them you would have to cross the ocean, and then climb a massive mountain, and underneath that mountain were six giant snakes. Danjoo also saw some strange creatures that he had never seen before. As soon as those creatures spotted any danger, they would make a strange noise to alert the alien king, who would then delegate his guards to eliminate the danger immediately.

Danjoo gathered people together revealed exactly what he saw in the vision. He asked us to accompany him in the quest to find Mami alive. We burst into laughter, because we thought that he was hallucinating and no one took him seriously. He cried with frustration that we would not believe him.

The next day, which was a Saturday, he wrote a bizarre letter, put it in a bottle and dropped it in the ocean:

Dear Saturday,

You are seen to be kind and humble. Your magnanimity towards my villagers has influenced them to serve you with respect and sincerity for many generations and I would never complain about that! But nonetheless, all that I remember about you is cruelty and dishonesty! And I am not angry for your incompetency or misjudgement which causes me to grieve and weep for many weeks! Saturday, you knew very well that Mami is my true love and I have manifested that in my actions! Thus, under your watchful eye I would kiss her twice on every Saturday, once in the morning and once in the evening, to ensure that my true love is well asserted and my real affection is well displayed to the world, without fear or contempt towards other women! Although you have witnessed this on many occasions, your ignorance towards my feelings and your misguidance towards a good judgment have allowed lust-filled men with brutal nature to take my shining star from the river of happiness to the mountain of destruction! Saturday, I will never forgive you for that. Despite my apprehension towards you and society, I would be content with only one favour and that is this: make sure that tonight, before you would hand over the day light to Sunday, kindly allow my Mami to see me in her visions and let her know that I do still love her and that one day I will be coming to rescue her from the alien king!

Danjoo

Again on Monday, he wrote a letter to Mami, and again he dropped the letter in the ocean, assuming that the waves would carry it to Mami wherever she was.

Dear Mami,

I knew exactly where you are and by God's grace next week I am coming to rescue you. But for now I am asking for your indulgence. I should have accompanied you to the beach on that day. However due to my stupid nature, I was not there to protect you. I wish I could turn back the clock but nevertheless I will do that when the time is

73

appropriate. I cannot describe the agony and the pain which I have gone through recently. I am sure it is not equal to the suffering and humiliation which you have endured in the past few weeks. Mami, I know that you think of me every day and that will never change under any circumstances. You belong to me and I am yours. I can smell your breath in the wind and I can test your feelings whenever I touch the water and until you return home safely, the little birds in town would continue to sing your name and even the clouds in the sky will never cease to remember you when it rains.

Mami, without the virtue of grief and sorrow, it would not be possible for lovers to build bonds. In the absence of tragedy, men would never discover their strength to create new empires. Heroes are not measured by their physical size but they are measured by how much they are willing to sacrifice for their lovers. I have long abandoned my obligations to mankind in order to serve my true love, which is you. I would assure you that I am entirely your servant, a servant who will never neglect his duties to serve a mistress who is worthy of his love until eternity.

I hope that Monday would never be cruel to me, like how Saturday ruined my soul, so that I can have a chance to smile again before I die. Mami, when I come to rescue you, I will shake the mountain like a tree and with my anger, I will boil the sea like a raging volcano and I will crush the alien kingdom like an angry elephant would trample on an ant. I will show no mercy to children, nor will I spare the women in the kingdom to mourn for the loss of their husbands. I will enslave the widows to become your servants in my new kingdom. And finally, Mami, I don't have to repeat that I love you! For now the blessings of the mighty would be sufficient to guide you and protect you.

Good night!

Danjoo

"What happened when Danjoo dropped the second letter in the ocean? asked Joseph.

"On that Monday, he returned home and locked himself in the house for six days without food only water. Then on Sunday, in the evening, he gathered the villagers once more and he sought their help to rescue Mami, but to no avail. At dawn the following day, Danjoo dressed from head to toe all in white and he rode on his father's horse with a jar full of water and a machete. Along with a dog which was called Laino, he embarked on his quest to rescue Mami, dead or alive.

We didn't suspected anything out of ordinary because usually in the morning he would ride a horse for hours and then he would return home. But on that day, nobody knew for certain where he went. It was his mother who alerted the villagers that Danjoo hadn't returned from his morning trip to the forest and we waited for a couple of hours, but when he failed to show up by sunset, it was then that we started a search and rescue.

The villagers separated into three searching teams: one group headed to the beach and they used canoes to search the ocean but they didn't see anything. The second team went searching in the surrounding villages and they didn't have any luck either. My group searched deep into the forest for a whole week and there was no sign of Danjoo and his dog.

Mysteriously, a few weeks later, Danjoo's horse came home safely, but Danjoo and Laino were nowhere to be seen. When the horse came back, some people suggested that we should return to the jungle to expand our search mission, so we did. On that occasion we encountered a strange monkey, which was making an odd noise. The monkey ran, and we ran after it, hoping that it would lead us to Danjoo somewhere deep in the forest, but it didn't.

After many hours in the bush, we reached a small river that we had never seen before and beside the river bank under a big tree, we found Danjoo's shoes and a white robe from the clothes which he was wearing on the day he went missing. But again there was no sign of him or the dog.

Since then, many years have passed, but villagers kept on having a vision that Danjoo and Mami were still alive. They must be living out there somewhere, and having a nice time together quietly but no one knows where that place is. I feel guilty about why I didn't accompany Danjoo to rescue Mami on the day he vanished. I have taken it upon myself to search for him until I die, and that is precisely why I am here."

The monk said his goodbyes, and left Joseph deep in thought.

5

Eventually Joseph returned from his holiday, and pretty soon a whole month had passed since Joseph and Grace had last spoken to each other. At that stage, he was really missing her. The story of Danjoo has impacted his life to the extreme, and he had become paranoid that what happened to Mami could have happened to Grace.

He decided at last to bite the bullet and went to her parents house. The moment Grace saw Joseph at the door, she ran to embrace him as if there had been no argument a month before.

"Darling, I felt like an idiot to leave you for a month without any form of communication." sobbed Joseph. "When I was away I learnt a lot about how to take care of my lover from stories told to me by Indians, by Africans and even in the Far East. I don't care what other people think, especially my dad and your friends, we are soul mates and we have to plan our future together. From now on I will work hard and save my money, then we must go to Burma and help villagers to search for Danjoo and his girlfriend."

Grace interrupted. "Who is Danjoo?"

"Well darling, it is a tragic story, but I will explain it to you fully later on. He was an innocent boy who went missing while he searched for his true love, and I am deeply troubled about it. I encountered a villager who witnessed the entire episode from A to Z. I have many bizarre love stories but Danjoo's story has affected me more than the others. In the future if we are bless with a child I would like to call him Danjoo.

Now, as you might know, my dad has again started a conversation concerning our baby. Can you imagine, darling, the minute I walked in the house, before I could even say hello to my mother, dad yelled at me 'Here we go again, another holiday, and when is your child due?' He is really annoying me and he is driving the family mad. Despite his awful behaviour towards me, my mother was quiet and she ignored him.

"Grace, we have only four months before our first anniversary. I cannot imagine you getting pregnant by then."

"Why can't we move out from your parents and rent somewhere?"

"Darling, we will struggle to afford rent in London, it is a very expensive city. Let's work hard and save our money, then we can travel overseas and search for Danjoo because I do really feel awful when I think of that innocent boy. He doesn't deserve that."

"But after what happened last time, I don't think my mother would allow me back in your house again, Joseph. She is extremely concerned about our welfare and there are too many conflicting stories about us circulating out there. She even sought help from a clairvoyant in the Midlands: that how bad it is right now. Too much has happened behind your back, but I have defended you with sincerity because I genuinely believed that whatever happened to us was not your fault. Your dad is a difficult man to live with. Are you truly sure that we are safe at your parents house, Joseph?"

"Of course we are, Grace! Don't worry about my dad. My mother will take care of us. I am profoundly convinced that my dad and my boss are extremely jealous of me because they never had the opportunity to travel the world like I do. It's precisely why they are jealous!"

"It's getting late now. Joseph. Go home and I will talk to my mum about it. And meanwhile you can also have a conversation with your mother, then we see what happens and I will catch up with you tomorrow at lunch time."

Joseph went home with mixed feelings, but straight after that, Grace rushed to consult her friend Dorisa. At Dorisa's house she dropped a bombshell.

"Dorisa, I need a favour. Joseph just left my house after a one month break. He was in the house for almost three hours. My mum wouldn't even say hello to him. She is still very angry about what his father did to us. I was frightened to offer him even a cup of tea. However, Joseph was adamant that I have to move back to his parents house, but I don't think my mum will ever allow that due to his father's abusive nature. But I do really want to go back to him because so many things are happening right now and I don't want Joseph to know those things." She burst into tears.

"Grace, why are you crying? Please tell me what is happening."

"You know that in our culture when you get married you must have a child by your first anniversary. Joseph's father is putting lots of pressure on us to have a baby as soon as possible, and we did our best but nothing is happening. While Joseph was away, I was desperate to get pregnant and I started to be naughty at work. One morning around 2 a.m. while I was alone at reception, a guy called Benjamin came downstairs and he approached me and complained that the air conditioning in his room was not working properly. I decided to go with him to look at the problem but the moment I entered in the room, he grabbed me from behind and he pushed me against the wall and started to kiss me all over. His hands were all over the place underneath my skirt and he was squeezing my breasts and grabbing my bottom. I felt really horny, then it happened."

"You meant you had sex with him?!"

"I didn't really mean to do it, Dorisa! It wasn't my fault, it just happened. He was so well-dressed and attractive, and since then we have been seeing each other every week."

"So you are having sex with Joseph while at the same time having another banana from outside! And who is Benjamin?"

"Um, really, I don't know much about him but his family lives in Copenhagen. He travels for business between London, Hong Kong and Singapore. He is one of our regular guests at the hotel. He is a white guy, tall, blue eyes, and he has long hair like a woman. He hardly speaks to anyone, he is always busy reading his newspaper or books. He looks rough but I have to admit that he knows how to look after a woman in bed. That is why I am dating him, not because of his money. You can call him a clown, I don't care! And I have something else to share with you confidentially, but not before you swear on your life that you will never tell anyone?

"Come on, Grace, we are friends for life, I would never share your secrets with anyone!"

"Well, I have a feeling that I am pregnant by him! I haven't seen Joseph for a month and I missed my period this month. So the child could be his or Joseph's, I don't know!"

"I beg your pardon? Are you serious that you are pregnant? I could never have imagined that you are capable of doing something like that! Are you out of your mind? Don't you worry about your reputation? Don't you worry about sexually transmitted diseases, Grace?"

"I just don't care, Dorisa, my body belongs to me!" Grace raged. "I can do anything with my body that I like and Joseph maybe guilty of doing the same thing as well because recently he has been mixing with all sorts of people: Indians, Chinese, African, Japanese, you name it. And how do I know that he is not having sex with other women behind my back? He went overseas alone without my knowledge and I don't know whether it was Cambodia, Nepal or Vietnam and he kept on moaning about some boy called Danjoo, that he felt sorry for."

81

"Who is Danjoo?"

"I don't have a clue! When I asked Joseph who he was, he kept saying we should talk about it later. He has even suggested that we have to work hard and save our money so that we can travel overseas and rescue this Danjoo. I think he is hallucinating. He is really annoying me, Dorisa, and I don't have time for all that! "

"What can I do to help you?"

"Can you have a word with mum please? I do really want go back to Joseph, and this is the right time for me because if I do go back now no one would suspect anything about my pregnancy. I can use our reunion as cover and continue with my life as normal. Even though our anniversary is fast approaching, when Joseph's dad finds out that I am expecting a child, that would tremendously ease the tension between us in the house. I know that Joseph's dad is a very arrogant fat man, and my mum too is a really stubborn lady and she is still very angry at Joseph and his dad for trying to tarnish my reputation. You know mum, she is old fashioned and if she finds out that I am pregnant out of wedlock, she will have a heart attack. It's guaranteed that she will kick me out her house and will have nowhere to live." Grace started to cry again.

"Don't cry, Grace, I will see what I can do to help you. Before I speak to your mum, promise me that you will stop having this affair with Benjamin. You cannot justify your actions! What you are doing is wrong, Grace. Joseph has done a lot for you and your family. He took you round the world and when you were accused of foul play in Las

Vegas, he stood by your side and defended you to the last minute and now you are cheating on him. I think Joseph is faithful and innocent and he will never cheat on you! If you don't stop cheating on your husband, you are going to be caught sooner or later!"

"Dorisa, it is not my fault. It is Joseph's dad's fault. If you push someone to deliver something which is beyond their human capacity, obviously they will do anything, even bad things, to achieve that. I was desperate to have a child by any possible means and Joseph has failed to make that happen for many months, then Benjamin comes along and bang, I'm pregnant. What is wrong with that, Dorisa? I told you in the past that sex with Joseph is not that great! I wish you could try Benjamin just for one night and then you'd know. He makes me feel like a woman and Joseph is quite useless at that. Joseph cannot even kiss me properly and he sleeps in my bed like a dead crocodile on the river bank. Do you really think that am doing this for pleasure? I am desperate for a child, aren't I?"

"Cheaters are great story tellers, Grace, and in my opinion you are no exception. It's just matter of time before someone at work will catch you red-handed with Benjamin!"

"Oh no, Dorisa, they will never catch us because we are so careful about it. And stop using the word "affair". We are not having an affair, we are just having a good time. We never go for a drink and we never go for dinner and we never talk to each other in the front of others. Usually he comes in late, and I pretend to my colleagues that I am going to use the bathroom, then I sneak into his room quietly and I jump in his bed then he would take care of my body for an hour or sometimes for two hours, then I go back to reception as if nothing has happened. For many weeks now, no-one suspected a thing and apart from you, I haven't told anyone."

"Nevertheless, they say no crime is perfect, and you should bear that in mind, Grace."

***

The next morning, Joseph's father confronted him with a chilling warning.

"Joseph, you are my first born, thus when I die you will be the primary beneficiary of my estate, including the house. However, I can see that you guys are not showing any respect for our values. We have only four months to your first anniversary and there is no sign of a baby. Grace is a bad girl and she is not interested in having a family with you. It's crystal clear that she has just been using you for money and she does not care about us and neither does she give a damn about our culture. You are wasting your money and energy like an idiot, travelling the world, and she is behind all that. A few weeks ago, Grace's friend told me that she has been taking birth control pills and that is precisely why she cannot get pregnant by you. You have trusted Grace too much and I told you on multiple occasions that never trust a woman too much otherwise she will stab you in the back, but you never listen. I am warning you for the final time, that you must get her pregnant in one month and if she fails to get pregnant, then

I will remove your name from my will and when I die, you will not receive any of your inheritance!"

"Dad, I am sick and tired of talking to you about Grace every day. She is the best wife I could ever have. You keep on complaining that I should not trust women, but dad, you trusted my mother and she is a woman."

"Do not compare your pious mother to that horrible girl! Your mother is one in a million. She is a lady with quality of character and she would never raise her voice above me or other members of my family! She respects our values and traditions, in contrast to that slag Grace!"

"Dad, be fair to me. Grace is a unique woman and she is one in a million too. She is loyal and understanding. I haven't talked to her for ages and yesterday when I visited her she was caring and understanding towards me. And we are planning to travel overseas to rescue Danjoo."

"And who is Danjoo?"

"Dad, he is a lovely boy who went missing in Burma while he searched for his true love. But the case is complex, you might not fully understand it anyway."

"Here we go again! Another fictitious character created by Grace! Joseph, you are a fool. I knew this would happen because whenever you go away, by the time you return home she always invents outrageous stories such as this in order to take you away from your family and waste your money doing crazy things just to appease her. I don't believe anything any more. In the past seven months since you got married, you have wasted thousands of pounds flying around the world like useless birds and you have neglected us and our values. I am going to repeat again: I give you just one month get her pregnant or I will kick you out of my house."

"Dad, let me tell you this. Grace has nothing to do with Danjoo and she does not use me for money at all. Dad, your generation and mine are quite different. You put lots of emphasis on family values and having children. To us, it is all about passion and pursuing our dreams. My passion is travelling and Grace is lucky to be my companion. If you recall that in the past before I even met Grace, how often would I beg you to take me overseas for sightseeing? Above all, I thought Grace's dad was your best friend and that is precisely why you arranged the marriage between us. Dad, if she is a bad girl, as you often argue, then why would you arrange a marriage between your son and the bad girl in town?"

"Joseph, I am not stupid! If she is innocent then show me the proof such as a news article related to the missing boy in Burma or a police report concerning the case. Besides, what has a missing boy got to do with you guys, other than a useless distraction? Indeed Grace's late father was my closest friend, and he was kind and honest, but I don't know anything about her. It was your mother who suggested her to me in the first place. If you are going to blame anyone, blame her, not me! You haven't realised that for days now, when people talk about you behind your back they don't have anything nice to say. Due to your clumsy nature, all your friends have abandoned you. And now, if I am to allow you to remain in my house, there will be no parties in here like before, and I need to see her pregnant as soon as possible. Is that clear or not?"

"Dad, please calm down. We won't be here for that long! I have my own plans anyway. I will talk to Grace about it and whatever we decide, I will let you know."

Grace and Joseph arranged to meet for lunch the very next day, to plan for the future.

"Oh Joseph, I am so excited that we can put our differences to one side and build an amazing future together."

"You know that I won't be able to live without you! You mean the world to me."

"My grandma used to say that there are two types of men out there: those who neglect their partners in the favour of public opinion and those who would stick with their lover no matter what. You have proven yourself to be the loyal one. And I know 100% that you will never hesitate to sacrifice your life for me if necessary, even if that means stabbing your father with a knife to get him out of the way, you will do it. And honey, guess what? While you were away, so many guys asked me out but I rejected every single one of them. I am not that type of woman who would jump into bed with different guys. I cannot lower my standards like that, Joseph. My friends were all jealous of me because I was the only virgin in our entire group and they were all cheap.

I bet you anything your dad has started moaning about the baby again. 'Joseph and Grace, where is the baby?'... as if I am a baby factory. This guy is really annoying and he is not a good Christian. He should understand that without the will of God we cannot have a child. That is the teaching of the holy bible. If God wills it, we can sleep together tonight and I could conceive tomorrow. Who knows, honey? I leave all my affairs in God's hands."

"Darling, how did you know that dad has started pestering me about the issue of the baby again? You are a genius this morning! We have had a massive argument about it. But I made it very clear to him that having a child right now is not a priority for us at the moment. He is threatening that if there is no sign of a baby by the end of the month he will remove my name from his will, which means that I will lose the house. But in the end, I convinced him to give us more time. I think it's okay now for you to return home. My mother can't wait to see you. Meanwhile I just need a little more time and freedom, hence I will have to leave my job and create my own online business. Then when I save enough money, we will travel overseas to rescue Danjoo. I don't see any future with my dad. Perhaps sooner or later we will have to rent a house elsewhere, far from here, in order to avoid a confrontation with him. But I am not sure about your mum! Do you still reckon that she will allow us to get back together again?"

"Yes, she will, for sure. I asked a few people to talk to her on our behalf and she has agreed to give your dad one more chance. But honey, I am more worried now than ever before. How can your dad remove your name from his will and deny you the right which only belongs to you? Honey, you have to do something about this because we cannot afford to lose that house. If you cannot have it then no one else should be able to! And Joseph, before I move back to your parents, let's go to Yorkshire this weekend, we need to sort ourselves out."

"OK Grace, I think that is good idea. But let me tell you this, am not really getting on with boss at work. I was absent from work several times and my boss didn't like that. I might lose my job. Right now I don't have much left in my savings account, so I need to create a small online business. If I lose my job we could then have something to rely on. I am going to see a business consultant now and I will catch up with you tomorrow."

6

A week later, Grace's friends Fiona and Dorisa met for coffee and Fiona asked Dorisa, "When was the last time you heard from Grace?"

"On Monday she came to my house and she begged me to talk to her mum, because her mum was quite reluctant to allow her to go back to Joseph's dad's house. She was really emotional about it and she cried like a child. We were supposed to meet the next day, but since then she kept on cancelling. This weekend she called to tell me that they were on their way to Yorkshire to see a business consultant. Apparently, Joseph plans to quit his job and start an online business soon. I don't know what to believe any more because Grace keeps on changing stories like she changes her socks."

"She is lying through her teeth! Do you know that she is having an affair with someone at work?"

"What? An affair? With whom?"

"One of her workmates. He's called Franklin and he is a mixed race guy from the Caribbean. She started seeing him five months after she got married to Joseph and since then they have been seeing each other almost every day. I tried to discourage her but she wouldn't listen. And guess what? I even approached Joseph to talk to him about it but he wouldn't listen to me. He was condescending towards me and said that when I married my Grace she was a virgin and that is very rare nowadays, and she is really loyal and faithful to me. A virgin! Ha! I was so angry. But anyway he is so dumb. He doesn't believe anyone but Grace. I bet you my life he is not blinded by true love: he is under her spell. Don't you know that Grace's mum is into Voodoo and black magic? She told me a long time ago that her mum went see a powerful spiritual healer living in the Midlands. And she was all "Oh, Fiona, I don't believe in that kind of rubbish", but look how she is controlling Joseph now. Is that normal?"

"Fiona, tell me more about this Franklin!"

"Well I've never met the guy but according to Grace he works in the hotel hospitality department and he plays music to entertain people in the hotel restaurant, and whenever he is around late at night they have sex in the rest room. Apparently she really likes him. At one point she even thought about leaving Joseph and marrying this guy and going to the Caribbean. Basically no one knows about it except me, because she is extremely secretive."

"Fiona, I can't resist the temptation not to share this with you! You know what? Grace is a prostitute, she is sleeping with all types of people. She never told me anything about Franklin, but she told me that she slept with a Danish guy called Benjamin and she might even be pregnant with his child! You see, that is precisely why I don't trust her any more.

She also told me a very strange story which is that next month Joseph is taking her overseas somewhere in the Far East in order to search for a boy who went missing while searching for his true love in the jungle. She even pretended that the whole idea was Joseph's, it has nothing to do with her and nobody knows anything about this boy. Do you actually believe that? No way!"

"You never know, she could be dealing with drug dealers in the Far East. I've heard many bizarre stories like that! Joseph is a dumb guy and Grace will take him to the cleaners. She will take him out there and somehow drug dealers would stuff his suitcase with Class A drugs without his knowledge and then he will bring the drugs into the UK.

And if he is caught, she will sell him out, like she did in Vegas. And then she can definitely marry Franklin and go to the Caribbean. So often it's the bad girls who are lucky and get the right guys. Joseph and his mother will do anything for Grace! He took her everywhere, she visited the most beautiful places on the planet that I would like to visit, and he bought her the most expensive jewellery, designer bags, you name it. How come at my age I can't even have a serious date? It is very unfair, Dorisa. Let's do something to ruin their marriage! I would suggest you record your conversation when you meet her next time and somehow try to trick her to reveal more about Benjamin and then I will give that recording to Joseph as a proof of her infidelity."

"Fiona, I agreed with you 100%. Somehow I will get her on record! I am baffled about her success. She is truly a lucky woman and she can get away with anything. She gets whatever she wants within seconds. Last week when I went to see her mum, I was pretty sure that she wouldn't allow Grace to go back to Joseph's but ironically when I opened my mouth about it, she goes "Oh, that is fine they are a happy couple, I don't mind, she can go back to him whenever she wishes" and I was really shocked because I was not expecting that. She was quite convinced that Grace will soon have a baby boy and the boy will be famous like a king and the whole world will know his name one day. Who on earth could predict such a wild dream? You are right, I am pretty sure that they put spells on Joseph and his mum!"

Three days later, Grace came to visit Dorisa with some news to share.

"Dorisa, we had an excellent time in Yorkshire, and I haven't had a good weekend like that for ages. We went shopping, had lots of intimacy, if you know what I mean? And I have some amazing news for you about Joseph's dad! Someone told me that he is visiting a brothel in the city and this is how he is doing it: during lunchtime, he takes the dog for walk. He leaves the dog at the vet, and then he would sneak into the brothel, which is behind the vet, and he would stay there for a while and then he would pick up the dog and go home. I am going to hire a private detective to spy on him and take photos and then I will use those pictures as a weapon against him. He is making our life hell and I will ruin his life too, I swear!"

Dorisa shouted at Grace. "Who told you this, Grace? I don't buy that story, they are lying! Your father in-law is a pious man. He goes to church every weekend and he is a respected member of society. He would never do something like that! Stop this character assassination, you are going too far now, Grace! Leave the old man alone. You must appreciate what he and his family have done for you but instead now you are tarnishing their reputation. That is horrible, Grace! I don't want know any more. If you are capable of doing this to your father in-law, you will never spare anyone, even me."

"Dorisa, you are acting like a drama queen. Stop being hysterical. It is my life. It has nothing to do with you! That fat man has ruined my life and he pushes me to the edge. Don't you feel sorry for us? Our only crime is that we love each other and we want to enjoy ourselves. What is wrong with that, Dorisa? I'm leaving!"

She slammed the door and headed straight home.

The next day Grace and Fiona met at lunch time in a bar.

"Fiona, I just wanted to let you know that that we have sorted out our differences and next week I will go back to Joseph's parents house. Recently he has quit his job and we are about to start our own online business, but he is insisting that we should travel overseas first."

"I am glad to hear that, but are you sure that you will get on with your crazy father-in-law?"

"Joseph told me not worry about him any more and we have decided to ignore him and carry on with our lives."

"Are you still seeing Franklin?"

"I don't want talk about my past! I am focused on building my future with Joseph."

"Where will you go next?

"We are going to the Maldives for seven nights and then we will go to Thailand for three days and then finally to Myanmar."

"Wow, I wish I could go with you. Can you afford all that at one go, Grace?"

"Oh yes, Joseph has some savings and my mother in-law gave us some money."

"Grace, can you be honest with me? What are you really doing in Thailand and Myanmar?"

"Well, it has been a while since we have been overseas so we decided to do it now before we start our new business. But Myanmar is different case altogether; Joseph has been there for a few nights and he met a Buddhist monk in a restaurant and he told Joseph a tragic story about a lost little boy called Danjoo. It has really traumatised Joseph and he want us to go there and search for the boy."

"Who is this Danjoo? Are you sure it's not a decoy for drug trafficking or human smuggling rings operating in the Far East? I have to be honest, to me that is what it sounds like! Your story doesn't make any sense to me."

"Fiona, what do you mean, drug trafficking and human smuggling? Do I look like a drug dealer or human smuggler? I can't believe that you too are acting like

Joseph's dad! Guess what, Fiona? I am extremely disappointed with everyone in my life at the moment because no one seems to understand me or my feelings. Yesterday I had a massive argument with Dorisa about my father-in-law and today you accuse me of dealing with drugs and human trafficking! Is it really worth having friends like you, Fiona? I've had enough and I am leaving."

"I am truly sorry if I've offended you with my silly remarks, Grace, I don't meant to hurt you. Forgive me, please! I was only joking."

They embraced each other.

"For some reason, Grace, you are so sensitive these days. When was the last time we had a good laugh? We can't behave like moody teenagers any more."

"I will arrange a lunch for three of us and then we can be silly again like there is no tomorrow!"

***

Two weeks later, Grace broke the good news to Joseph.

"Joseph what would you do if I told you that I am pregnant? I was supposed to have my period last week, but I didn't, and I tested myself today. It's positive!"

"Oh darling, you are kidding me! Finally you are what? Pregnant! Oh my God, now I am truly a believer and miracles do happen! And I can't wait to share that news with my parents."

"Um no… no.. no, Joseph, wait for a month just to be on the safe side?"

"No, darling, I can't wait any longer, my dad thinks that I am useless and I won't be able to make you pregnant and I have proved him wrong! I can't wait to share that news with the whole world and then we can start celebrating as soon as possible!"

With euphoria and massive excitement, Joseph informed his parents and they too were so happy about it. The next few weeks were the happiest weeks for the family since Joseph and Grace got married.

7

To everyone's surprise, a week later Vladimir organised a surprise party for Grace and Joseph at their home. He invited Grace's family and friends as well as their co-workers to attend. At the dinner table, he stood and made a speech.

"I am delighted that soon I am not only going to be a dad, but a grandfather too. In our culture, it is extremely important to keep the family line going. I am nearly 70 years old and with my current state of health, I might not be here for long. But I know that now, even if I was to die tomorrow, my family line will continue through my grand children. Grace and Joseph, from now on you can do whatever you like and I will not complain any more, even if you fly to space. I don't care!" And everyone laughed.

But there was more. "Joseph, your mother told me that you guys plan to visit the Maldives and Thailand for your anniversary in October, however, this time around you don't have to worry about the cost. I will take care of everything." Everyone in the room applauded.

"Wow, Dad, thank you very much, we are really grateful", said Joseph.

Grace chimed in. "May God reward you for your generosity. We were not expecting that at all!"

"Oh no that is fine, you don't have to thank me! From day one, I made a promise to God that when Joseph's wife conceived, I would organised a surprise party and I would give you air tickets to fly to wherever you wish. I am fulfilling my promise."

"Grace, we are really looking forward to welcoming our grandchild into the family," said Merry. "And the reason why my husband kept on moaning about 'no baby' was the pressure from our culture. As you know, our culture dictates that when a couple gets married the wife must get pregnant by their first anniversary otherwise the husband has the right to marry a second wife. And if your first born is a girl, the wife would control the affairs of your family and if it is a boy, then the husband does."

Then Grace's little sister Elizabeth piped up "What if they are twins?", and everyone laughed.

"Oh my dear, we never actually thought about that before!" Again everyone laughed. "Joseph is my first born, hence my husband had to control our family affairs. But people who don't understand our culture properly thought that I was a weak woman and I am too obedient to my husband, like a slave. It's important that you guys learn more about our culture in order to avoid misunderstandings in the future. Do you have any baby names in mind, Joseph?"

"Of course I do, mum! If it's a boy we will call him Danjoo, and if it's a girl we will name her Mother Theresa!" and the room melted with laughter.

"What if they ARE twins? What will you call them?"

"If they are two boys, we will name one after my late father and the other for Joseph's dad," said Grace. "If they are two girls, we will call one Mary, the mother of Jesus, and the other Mary Magdalena his disciple. And if it is a boy and girl, then we will give them our own names: Joseph junior and Grace junior."

Elizabeth wasn't satisfied "How about my name? Why wouldn't you call her Elizabeth? It's more posh than Grace."

"Grace sounds more modern and Elizabeth is an old fashioned name," teased Joseph.

"Oh shush, you. Anyway, Grace, when are you due?"

"Elizabeth, you ask too many questions. I am not 100% sure, it could be February or March next year!"

"But I thought if you have a child in February, it can be bad luck?"

Vladimir decided to put her straight. "Oh, that is superstition. As devout Christians we don't believe in things like that! Having a baby is a blessing from God: he knows best and we don't. God does everything for a reason."

"But my mum says that there is a good time and a bad time for everything. And that there is a good place as well as a bad place for everything!"

Vladimir laughed and said "Well, our good time is here and now and your good time is tomorrow and in the future! You are really a smart girl and I like your questions."

***

A few weeks went by and Joseph noticed that his wife was looking more and more depressed.

"Darling, what's wrong?"

"Honey, I am going through hormonal changes. I don't feel like doing anything and I don't have an appetite either. I keep on vomiting every day but the doctors say it is normal to feel like that. Maybe I need to change the weather and see what happens."

"I reckon you should quit your job and help me run this business, bearing in mind that my dad's generation and ours are quite different. They are greatly influenced by popular culture and society and I am not going to be ruled by society norms. Even though he is behaving himself very well at the moment, you cannot predict what he's going to do and I won't accept any further pressure from him. Because your pregnancy came late, he might still suggest that I should marry a second wife, but I am not interested in marrying other women. I love no one but you.

My friend Bob said that when we go overseas next month, you can come home after our visit to Thailand, and I can go to Myanmar by myself and search for Danjoo. You're pregnant and it will be safer for you to be at home. I do agree with him, but what do you think?"

101

"Joseph, that sounds like a good idea, because I think I will have to consult a doctor to make sure that it is safe for me to fly. I don't mind leaving my job so I can look after your business if that would make you happy."

"While I'm in Myanmar, mum and dad will take care of you and there would be no argument concerning the second wife. My dad's attitude is quite different to mine. He is selective about who to love and who to associate with. Often they are judgmental of people who are a different colour or religion. I am really the opposite.

When I was a child I had a yoga class and I learnt this from the monk: love is more powerful than hate. If someone is horrible and means to you, you should show them kindness and generosity. If you share with the poor and the needy, surely God will take care of all your affairs. Don't judge people based on their colour or religion rather judge them on the quality of their character. Never hold a grudge against anyone, forgive wrong doers as much as you can and let God punish them.

My perception of humanity has profoundly changed. Danjoo is now dearer to me than my own brother. I am a citizen of the world and thus precisely I get along with Indians, Africans, Chinese, and Europeans. I relate to other people's pain and whenever I think of Danjoo, it genuinely reminds me of you. If someone kidnapped you and took you deep into the ocean like they did to Mami, what would happen to me? I have a moral and sincere obligation to rescue him if I can."

***

At home, Elizabeth talked to her mother.

"Mummy, are you sure that Grace will be fine at Joseph's house? She looks sad and confused. I have been there twice this week but she was sleeping all day. And when she woke up, I talked to her but it was like talking to the wall. She was withdrawn from everyone, and even Joseph has started to wonder why. That is not the Grace that we know! Ask them to allow her to come home until she has the baby."

"Calm down, Elizabeth, she will be fine. A first-time pregnancy is often accompanied by mixed feelings and anxiety. Different people react in different ways, especially if the baby is a boy. I have experienced similar symptoms before. Besides that, she has just left the job that she loves the most and their online business is not doing well at all. It will be a frustrating time for them."

"Mummy, how do you know that her unborn child will be a boy?"

"Someone told me a long time ago that her first born will be a boy and I believe so.

"I'm not so sure. She has changed and it has nothing to do with her pregnancy. Something is not right with Grace, I am really concerned about her well-being. At least she is now being getting on well with her father-in-law. He seems a very nice man. I hope my future father-in-law will be a kind man like him."

"Elizabeth, doctors say that early pregnancy often comes with health problems, but it doesn't mean that Grace is in danger."

"OK, mum, now that you have spelled everything out for me, I feel better about it."

***

However, Grace's friends were still plotting and scheming.

"Dorisa, I told you that Grace was making up stories about her father in-law, but it seems they were just stories."

"Fiona, her father-in-law is so generous. He seems so calm. It's hilarious that she is blessed with these marvellous people looking after her, but she is so spiteful sometimes. I can't believe that they worship her."

"I told you, black magic has engulfed Joseph's family and Grace's mother will never stop using it."

"Grace is unusually quiet at the moment. Perhaps she is planning her next move. She is clever and cunning. She keeps on complaining that we are jealous of her, but we are not, we are just stating the fact as they are! It's not fair that we are the good girls. She is the bad one and she is living a dream life. Over my dead body, I will never allow that to continue! And I will find a way to inform her useless husband that the child is not his."

8

Two days before Joseph and Grace went to the far East, Grace and her mother met for dinner.

"Grace, I visited the African guy in Wolverhampton and I asked him to do a reading for you."

"Which guy?"

"My friend, the astrologer from Africa."

"Oh, mum, you are at it again!"

"No, let me tell you what he said. He said that your child will be a boy, he will be extremely famous and popular, and one day he will rule the world like a king. Also, according to him, you have a dark secret which you are hiding from us, but soon I will find out what it is, and he made a chilling prediction that before you give birth, there will be deaths in the family: a man and a woman.

In order to avoid future confrontation with your father-in-law, he asked me to kill a white cow on a Friday and share the meat among the poor and the needy. I gave him the money to do the sacrifice on our behalf. And he gave me this powder to give to you. You must mix that powder with tea and then give it to Joseph and when he drinks it, he will love you even more. And here's something which you need to carry with you wherever you go. It will keep you safe from your enemies, because according to him you have too many enemies out there! I am really concerned about your safety overseas because he predicted that while you are abroad someone may die. You should cancel your trip!"

"Mum, for God's sake, stop wasting your money on this rubbish. Are you out of your mind? If this guy is as powerful as you think, then why doesn't he sort out the mess in his own country? In Africa, people are dying every day from hunger, senseless wars, malaria and poverty."

"Grace, shut your mouth! In this country, how many doctors are dying from a terminal disease? If they can cure other people why don't they cure themselves first? God gives you the power to help others and equally others use their power to help you; that is how it is supposed to be."

"Mum, we are flying out in two days time! It's too late to cancel my trip, and we would lose lots of money. We cannot really afford that. Whatever is going to happen, let it happen. I am sick and tired of such rubbish, and right now I have too much going on in my mind. Our love is genuine and it will naturally grow from strength to strength.. Anyway, if you insist, give me that mumbo jumbo stuff. It's getting late and I have to go."

"Grace, are you really sure it is safe to fly? I think it's against medical advice to fly within the first twelve weeks of your pregnancy!"

"Mum, I don't have any complications and I will be fine."

"OK, I'm not happy about it but I wish you a safe journey."

"I love you, mum. Bye."

***

After 11 hours in the sky, finally the happy couple safely landed in Malé. In the next seven days, Joseph and Grace spoiled each other like never before.

"Honey, it's an incredible adventure for us to be here. We are really having fun!"

"Of course, darling, this island is a paradise for lovers. The beaches are magnificent and the people are unique. Just have a look at some of those hotels out there built in the middle of the ocean."

"Joseph, I noticed that the culture of the indigenous people here is pretty similar to that of Indians living in East London. It appears as if they share the same family tree and traditions."

"Yep, thousands of years ago, this island was part of the Indian continent. You know what, when I look down into the ocean, it reminds me of Danjoo and Mami."

"Darling, off you go again. Please stop. We are not here to grieve, we are here to enjoy ourselves like free-spirited teenagers. I want to have as much fun as I can, but you can mope about your Danjoo as much as you wish."

"Darling, I heard that there is a beautiful mosque somewhere here which is almost five hundred years old. I think we should go there and seek a blessing for our unborn child."

"Honey, you're too much like my mum with your spirituality, and you know what I think about that. First let's find out where to eat and where to do our shopping. That's more important than your fairy tales. Just remember that God is always with you as long as you have a good heart."

"Now you are the preacher and I am your disciple!"

"Joseph, my grandma often used to say that true lovers educate each other in a foreign land, because they never learn anything at home, and men are the best teachers in the foreign land and if you educate one woman you have educated the entire world. On this holiday I am truly eager to learn a lot from you.

Changing the subject, my friend Dorisa suspects that her partner has been cheating on her but she is not sure about it. What are the signs which indicate that a partner is cheating?"

"Wow, darling, this is precisely why I love you. You always ask such great questions. I have read lots of romantic books and watched blockbuster movies about deception in relationships and cheating is the cause of every single tragedy.

I can't say why people cheat in the first place, because absolutely every case is different. There are lots of reasons for it: some are genuine while others only God knows. Different cultures take different approaches on the true meaning of cheating. Some make sense while others don't. But here are the two main signs: when they started to lie constantly, and when they start to be unusually secretive."

"Some reasons for cheating may be good ones? How does that work?"

"For example, if your husband is impotent and he is in denial about it, then his wife could be tempted to have sex elsewhere. Equally if the woman has a phobia about sex but doesn't admit it to her husband, then probably he would have little choice but to eat someone else's apple."

"How about if your husband often makes a joke about how other women look, is that also a sign?

"Well, joking about something could be a way to hide true feelings, and could be a sign that someone is lying."

"If someone has cheated on their husband, what would be the best way to confess it?"

"Darling, there is no good way to confess about cheating. There will be bad consequences! However, there might be a better place and time to confess."

"When would that be?"

"Maybe on your death bed. It is the only place and time where you can whisper to your spouse 'Oh, my angel, I have not been entirely faithful to you and I am sincerely guilty about it! I am asking forgiveness from you.' Darling, the moment that people start cheating is exactly that moment they impose a life sentence upon themselves, and the day that they confess about it is the day they have declared a death sentence upon themselves."

Grace yawned rather rudely and said "Honey. it is bed time now. let's go to bed."

"Darling, that is not fair, I want to learn from you too. Tell me what are the signs to indicate that your husband is cheating?"

"Honey, I have too much going on in my mind right now. That is why I can't think straight. But often I have heard that if a man keeps on comparing his wife to other women, or if he keeps on complimenting her for no obvious reason, such a guilty sign could be a pattern of cheating. But I would be able to tell, by my instincts."

"You mean if I cheat on you, your instincts will tell you?"

"Exactly."

"Then using your instincts, have I ever cheated on you?" Grace laughed but Joseph pressed her for an answer. "Just be honest, darling, what would you do if I cheated on you?"

"I would eat you alive! How about you honey, would you ever forgive me if I cheated on you?"

"Grace, I was clear when I spelled out everything. I give my verdict on behalf of all men."

"I don't care what other men think, I am talking about you."

"Darling, let me repeat again, all cheaters deserve to be strangled."

"So you mean that if I ever cheated on you, even if it is not my fault, you will kill me?"

"Well, darling, I will leave that to your imagination!"

And with massive shock, Grace rushed to the bathroom and she was sick into the toilet for a while. Joseph reacted as if nothing was happening and he continued to read his book. Grace tried to get his attention but she failed, so quietly she lay down on the bed and pulled the covers over her head.

In the middle of the night, all of a sudden, Grace jumped from the bed and screamed out loud. "Joseph! Joseph, please wake up. Help me, I can't breathe."

Joseph leapt up from a deep sleep and shouted "What is wrong with you Grace? Are you okay?"

"I was having a nightmare," she said. "I saw dead bodies and I saw a horrible face looking at me like a zombie and he was going to attack me. It's your fault, Joseph, you should never talk about death to me. It petrifies me."

"Darling, calm down, I didn't mean to scare you. What else did you see in your dream?"

"I saw a group of men fishing at the river bank, then a tall guy arrived from nowhere and people ran to welcome him and they said that he was Benjamin Franklin."

"That is brilliant. My mother once told me that if a pregnant lady saw a noble person in her dream, it is a sign that she will have a boy. And Benjamin Franklin was a noble man, which means it is a blessing for us."

"Who was he?" Grace asked.

"Benjamin Franklin was one of the founding fathers of America. When we were in Vegas, you saw his portrait on the $100 bill many times."

"But seeing dead bodies in a dream is not a good sign at all, honey."

"Oh darling, it is just a nightmare." Eventually the two of them managed to get back to sleep.

The next five days for the young couple in the Maldives was like paradise on earth. They spent time sightseeing, eating out at different restaurants, shopping like never before and they swam like crocodiles.

"Honey, this is the best holiday that we have ever had. On our previous holidays, your dad was always at the back of my mind, but not now. I wish we could stay here forever. What do you think?" Grace asked.

"Absolutely, you are spot on, but I think we are going enjoy Thailand even more than here, because the night life in Bangkok is terrific."

"How many hours to fly from here to Bangkok?"

"Well, with good weather, about four hours."

"OK. Hey, put aside your book, we need to talk. Honey, when people describe somebody as kind but with a dark side, what comes to your mind?"

"Perhaps he is a child molester or a paedophile or even a serial killer."

"What about adultery?" she asked.

"Grace, we are all sinners."

"What is the ideal wife that you will prefer for your son?"

"Maybe a woman who has qualities like my mother."

Grace was surprised. "I didn't expect that, honey, I thought that you would say that I would be the ideal wife, not your mother!"

"Darling, our generation is quite different. My mother knows the true meaning of marriage and companionship and we don't. And you cannot value something if you don't actually know what it means. To us having fun and material value is everything, and that is not right. God does everything for a reason. When we broke up, I learnt a lot about family values, the role of parents in society, and the complex affairs of human beings. Can I also ask you, darling, what do you really worry about? Lately you have being asking many weird questions. Are you being unfaithful to me?"

"Don't ask me such a ridiculous question, Joseph! Am I capable of doing something awful like that? Remember that I was a virgin when you married me!"

"Darling, people can change like the weather. Being a virgin doesn't meant anything to anyone any more. It's like when people brag that 'I am a devoted Muslim' or 'I am a devoted Christian', it doesn't mean anything."

"You may think that I am silly, but I ask these questions because I am confused. When we have a conversation now it felt as if I am talking to a scientist, not my husband. At the moment you are cool towards me and you hardly show me any affection and you are not behaving like a father who is expecting a child. Before I was pregnant, all that mattered to you was me: you worshipped me as if I was a goddess, but now you are selfish and distracted. Your books and computer are your true love, and not me."

"Grace, you reckon that I am selfish and distracted: well, maybe that is true. But equally you are unusually evasive and hyper-defensive and that is not helpful either. It only suggests one thing to me, and I wonder if you are being entirely honest with me! Perhaps my thoughts have slightly shifted from you to Danjoo, but your behaviour is far worse than mine and you know that but you won't admit it. Of course before, it was all about you, but now I have you on my mind and I have my business on my mind, and I have Danjoo on my mind, and on top of that, we are expecting a child in February. Above all I have to prove myself to my dad who thinks that I am incompetent. I am only one man and I have a million things going through my mind. My interaction with people from different backgrounds has truly expanded my horizons. True lovers like us should never break up. We must try to sort out our differences amicably before it is too late. If we don't, things will never be the same."

"What is your biggest regret so far?"

"My failure to listen to my father."

"Not our separation?" she asked.

"Not really," he said. "Had I genuinely listened to my father's advice, we would never have separated in the first place and we would be the happiest couple that ever lived. Instead of all these distractions, we could have tried harder to have a child and then focused on building a healthy relationship with my family."

"I wish I had never given in to your father's pressure to get pregnant. I totally disregarded mum's advice. I was paranoid about you getting a second wife, and that has significantly messed up my life big time. I've done some stupid things, and if I knew then what I know now, perhaps I would have let you have a second wife, and returned half of your dowry.

But at the same time, I am not prepared to accept that. Can you imagine me sharing you with another woman? No way. Because we are soul mates! When you left and disappeared into your fantasy world, out of desperation, my mum went mad. She consulted that ridiculous spiritualist, which she thought would make us happy and I never used to believe in those things, but if you're desperate you will believe anything."

"Darling, we are soul mates, and there will be no second wife. If we had listened to our parents right from the start we could have avoided all this confusion.

But good things take time and we are making progress now. It is only a caring father that would pay a fortune just to put a smile on a young couple's face, taking into account that my mother is suffering from heart disease. They want see us happy, that is why he is doing this. However the biggest mission for me to accomplish now is to travel to Myanmar and search for Danjoo and when I return safely then we will live happily ever after."

"Darling, when get to Bangkok, I have a surprise for you."

"Are you serious?"

"Yes. It is a bombshell though, and the impact may equal the big bang. And I hope that after that we can forgive each other and then make our future great again."

"Just give me a hint about it!"

"Honey, I can't! Just wait until we reach Bangkok. It has something to do with Benjamin Franklin."

"Wow, I can't wait to hear it!" And they kissed each other.

9

The exotic aromas of Bangkok and the melting pot of Asia was the next playground for Joseph and Grace. A few hours after arrival the couple activated party mode and quickly swung in to action.

"Honey, I have never seen such exciting people as Thais in my entire life. I think tonight we should go clubbing and be crazy!"

"I wouldn't take you to a night club, you are pregnant, for God's sake!"

"Oh Joseph, really? I want to experience the night life."

"I think we should ride the tourist bus tomorrow and view the city from all angles. The next day we can go into the mountains and look at the Thai scenery."

"Honey, don't forget about the beach, I love swimming."

"Grace, this is not the Maldives. Beaches are many hours away from Bangkok."

"Oh I see. I saw on a TV documentary that this city is full of pickpockets, but so far I haven't seen anything like that. People seem really nice. We may even enjoy it more here than the Maldives. Honey, what would you compare this crowd to? Look how busy it is. It reminds me of rush hour at Victoria station. I hope we are not going to lose our way back to the hotel, it is truly messy here. Wow, look at those bicycle taxis diving through the traffic like clowns. I wonder if there are any traffic rules here? I reckon we should ride one of those taxis and be crazy like everyone else. They seem quicker than a vehicle. Too much traffic in town and vehicles are growing like babies. Hey, let's find somewhere to eat, I am ready for a break."

"Okay honey, let's eat here. I am going to have seafood, and what about you?"

"Darling, let's eat from one plate like we are twins."

"For me South Asia is all about delicious food. And guess how much all this food costs, including our drink? 500 Thai Baht, which is nothing." said Joseph.

"That is why you put on weight when you went to Myanmar and I kept on telling you to lose the weight on your stomach. It is not really healthy for you."

"Ha! Don't mind about my belly, I am pregnant too and I will give birth soon. If you make fun of my belly, just wait for a while, yours will start hanging out soon as well. Grace, do you have any change with you?"

"Yes, I have."

"Can you please give to that lady who is begging?"

"Joseph, there are too many poor people hanging out here. If you start giving out money you could attract unwanted attention. Please let's eat quietly and ignore the beggars for now."

"Are you really sure about that, honey? It seems mean."

"Yes, I am."

"Okay, if you say so."

"Honey, I've had enough now. I think we should go back to the hotel and relax. I can smell something which is very unpleasant and I feel like vomiting. When you're pregnant, if you see anything spicy, you crave it, but when you eat it, you feel like being sick."

"Then let's jump in a taxi and go back to our hotel. Do you still want to go to a night club tonight? Are you still okay about that? If you don't I will go by myself."

"I don't think I will go any more but it's okay by me if you want to go after the Thai ladies, you go!"

"Don't be silly, darling, I'm not interested in Thai ladies. You know that I am a party animal and I like going to clubs to enjoy myself, that is all. I am blind to other women. Please don't feel jealous. I will behave myself."

"Go and have fun. I bet you anything my mum and your dad are extremely worried about why we haven't called them. She even suggested that I should cancel this trip. She is so protective."

"Sometimes you must allow people to wonder. We've never had an opportunity to have a great time like this before, and it will be a miracle if we ever do something amazing like this again. We are expecting a child and when you become a parent, everything changes. Pretty soon it will be no longer about us, but our children. However for now it is all about sex, drugs and rock and roll. High five, Grace!"

"Well, I guess you are right. We must take lots of pictures so we remember it. I am still upset that when we got robbed in the Vegas those good memories vanished into thin air. Just look at the beauty of the Thai people, their food, the bustling city, full of bicycle taxis. If I told my sister about this, she wouldn't believe it and you cannot blame her. Honey, make me laugh. No one does Michael Jackson's Thriller dance better than you. Show me how he does the robot!"

"Oh, you mean like this? Or hands up in the air, butt swinging from left to right? Clap along with me, I am Michael Jackson!"

"Honey, you are so funny, look how the taxi driver is staring at you. He must think we are weirdos!"

The happy couple couldn't get enough of each other. Somehow Thailand re-ignited the couple's chemistry, and the next few days was about partying, intimacy, sightseeing, shopping, dining, and clubbing. The weather was fantastic, the blue sky was happy to give them opportunities and the sun was willing to shine for them. For Joseph and Grace nothing mattered apart from having fun.

But the night before Joseph departed for Burma in the pursuit of the mysterious boy, at dinner, Grace once again tried to convince him to abandon his outrageous plan.

"Honey, what time are you leaving tomorrow?"

"From here to Myanmar is only one hour by air, but I am using the night bus. I want to blend in with the locals, but don't worry, in the afternoon I will drop you at the airport. Then I'll catch the night bus from here to Yangon. It will only take a few hours."

"Darling, you know that I don't feel good about this at all. My instinct is telling me something. You are going to Myanmar alone without proper medical insurance. Aren't you worried about malaria, TB and typhoid? Are you really sure that you are doing the right thing, Joseph? It is will to be a miracle if you find him. Is it really worth it to try such crazy stuff?"

"Darling you believe in your instincts and I worship mine too! I am called to action by a divine power and nobody should actually dispute that. I die in the struggle so be it! Anyway, I am still waiting to hear your surprise about Benjamin Franklin. Are you going to share that with me tonight?"

"Honey, you don't have to raise your voice, it is alright, you can go, it is your life. But about Benjamin Franklin.. I have changed my mind about telling you about that. However last night while you slept, I wrote a letter which contains the full story and when I say good bye to you at the airport, I will hand it to you. But do not open it, please, until you reach Myanmar. When you have successfully rescued Danjoo, on that day kindly open the envelope while you sit next to him. I am reluctant to give it to you unless you swear on your mother's life that you are going honour my wishes."

"Darling, I have been honouring your wishes right from day one, and I will always do so!"

"Good boy. I know that you will behave yourself and that is why you're my hero." They kissed.

"Do you know where you are staying in Yangon?"

"Oh, not yet, darling, but I will call you and give you my contact details as soon as I know. Wish me luck. When you get back to London, do your best to meet up again with Precious. She is your only true friend right now. Fiona and Dorisa have gone behind your back to colour your name many times. They called you greedy and selfish, but I totally gave them a deaf ear. I am warning you about them."

"Honey, I have suspected that for a while now. Thank you for being so concerned."

The next day. At 2 p.m. at Bangkok International, Joseph and Grace hugged each other goodbye and she gave him the letter as promised. Grace flew back to the UK and Joseph went on his way to Myanmar. In the first possible quiet moment, sitting alone on the flight, he tore open the letter, and this is what he read:

Dear Joseph;

I don't know where to begin or where to end! But with your kindness and genuine understanding of my feelings, I hope you will forgive me if I express myself until I run out of ink. You may recall that in the past two weeks I have been borrowing your dictionary. I did that because I was looking for a word which is sufficient to precisely describe my despicable behaviour but so far I can't find any words which could truly satisfy my broken ego. My hands are trembling with shame and guilt.

First let me thank you for the gentle courtesy which you have accorded to me at all times. I would like to thank you for all the good things which you have done for me and my family and may God bless you always. Last year when my dad died, I thought that no one would ever put a smile on my face again but you have proved me wrong. The day that you married me, you transformed my life from a useless girl in the ghetto who was heading nowhere to a princess like Lady Diana.

To cut a long story short, Joseph, I am not the same pious girl that you met last year. Out of desperation I became a woman who lost her self-worth. I did something which is far worse than prostitution. Joseph, I have cheated on you, not once, not twice, but many times, with two different guys. First I slept with one of the guests in the hotel, Benjamin from Denmark, and again with one of my colleagues, Franklin from the Caribbean. Joseph, you gave me the opportunity to take this secret with me to my grave but I have no desire to do that. I have to confess now, because the burden of guilty is no longer bearable for me to carry on my shoulders.

The shame that I endure every day is beyond imagination. I have thought many times about how to reveal my sins to you but I couldn't find the heart or the words. Joseph, there was no justification for my actions whatsoever and the shame that I brought on our families is beyond repair. I have been evasive and aggressive. My mum, a pious lady, has done her best to guide me and straighten me up but my ego engulfs me with too much pride and thoughts of vengeance. And now I am suffering the consequences.

The saddest thing for me now is that the child that I am currently carrying in my womb may not be yours after all. Joseph, I would like to have a DNA test when you return and if it proves that this child is yours, that would be a great relief for me. I can assure you that if it is not yours, I will offer him or her for adoption, then I will commit suicide. Joseph, you may notice odd stains on the paper which you are reading now ,with ink flowing everywhere. There are grieving tears running down my cheeks like a waterfall. Once again I am so sorry!

Joseph, you know that I have never prayed to God before, but now I will ask him to soften your heart so that you can forgive me, and if not, let him take my soul quietly while I sleep.

I am asking for your forgiveness and I ask you to give me one more chance in order to prove to the world that I have regretted my awful past.

Joseph, genuine heroes are not men who would kill sinners, but they are men who would swallow their pride and forgive a lustful wife when she has committed a sin and transgressed against the Almighty. If you don't forgive me, I will respect that. A caring husband like you and a pious son who carries noble blood from a great family does not deserve to marry a dirty woman who is deceitful, selfish and greedy. I am not worthy any more to be called darling, just call me Grace. I will not call you honey, but Joseph. Those loving words genuinely belong to women who are loyal, honourable, pious and faithful. Sorry, my dear, I am lost and I can't write any more. I'm sorry for ruining your life and sorry for breaking your heart.

10

In London, Fiona and Dorisa met for lunch.

"I saw Grace last night and she looks gorgeous," Fiona said. "She talked about how beautiful Thailand was, the people and the food and what have you. I can't believe that she looks happier than usual. I bet you Joseph still hasn't found out what she did behind his back. We have to work out how to reveal her secret to Joseph's dad before Joseph comes back. I searched the internet for the story about this Danjoo kid but I couldn't find anything. The name Danjoo is more common in Tibet and Cambodia than Burma. I told you it was a cover story for something dodgy.

Someone told me that Westerners like Joseph are now involved in the human trafficking rings operating in the Far East. It is a lucrative business. They marry women from poor countries like Thailand, Cambodia, Vietnam and Myanmar, and then they apply for a spouse visa and pretend they were genuine couple, then they smuggle these women into Japan, Hong Kong and South Korea. People are making a fortune out of it. £10,000 to £20,000 every month!"

"Yes, Fiona, I told you he was capable of drug peddling. He hangs out with dodgy people from different backgrounds and Grace is a key player in all that. She pushes him to do anything which serves her purpose. It is intriguing that they recently started a new business with little capital. It gives them a perfect motive to raise funds by any means necessary. Joseph is useless. He wouldn't be able to run a sophisticated business like that and she doesn't have the brain to manage such a business either. She is only good at giving her body to useless men."

"But how shall we approach her father-in-law with this evidence?"

"Apart from Grace, Joseph's family only trusts Bob, his best friend. We have to show Bob the evidence and then somehow convince him to share it with Joseph's dad."

"Bob is a very straight up guy, I don't think he would be involved in something like this. Bob thinks Grace is amazing. Here's what you should do. Write a letter, and wear gloves so that you don't leave any finger prints on it. Then sometime next week after my hospital appointment, we can go to their house at midnight and then drop the letter in their letter box. Then we will see what happens."

"But what if Grace picks it up?"

"Oh no, she wouldn't do that, her father-in-law collects all their letters. Remember when he received that package on behalf of Joseph and when he opened it he discovered the air tickets to Dubai and he nearly had a heart attack about it?"

"Yes, I do remember. Awesome, so let's do that next week."

"Alright, I am going back to work, Have a great weekend, Fiona!"

***

A few days later, Grace decided to pay Precious a surprise visit. She knocked at the door and it opened.

"Do you still remember my name, Precious?"

"Who is that? Oh my God, I am not going to call you Grace any more. I call you a stranger!" They hugged each other. "Where have you been, darling? I guess it is the same as usual: holidays and parties like there is no tomorrow. I called you several times but you have been constantly ignoring my phone calls and you don't return my texts either."

"Oh, it is a long story, but anyway, how are you? Your house looks really messy, are you doing some renovations at the moment?"

"Yes we are putting an extension at the back and the house needs decorating too, but there is more to it. Something else is coming up soon, but am not going to tell you right now. I don't have to ask what you like to drink, because I know your choice, so let me make you a cup of tea and we can chat."

"How is your mum and your fiancée?"

"Mum is not too bad and she keeps on asking about you, answered Dorisa. "However, I have some good news and some bad news. The good news is that Stuart and I will get married in January. The bad news is that I might lose my job in two months time, because starting next month there will be redundancies at work. Our major customer is not

128

going to renew our contract any more because now they are shifting more from handsets towards home broadband hence land lines are no longer attractive to their clients. So am going to be jobless soon, I think."

"I am sorry about that. But congratulations on your upcoming wedding. I am really excited that finally you will tie the knot with Stuart. Are you looking forward to married life?"

"Of course I am, I can't wait."

"Fingers crossed that your father-in-law is not like mine! My life is ruined, Precious." Grace sobbed her heart out.

"What happened, Grace?"

Grace slowly revealed everything about Benjamin and Franklin.

"Guess what, Grace? I suspected something like that for long time but I wasn't sure with whom. You were very clever at hiding it, but also people are not stupid. They could tell something was going on. I did warn you quite a few times but you thought that I was jealous of you. People do cheat in relationships and most people are guilty of it, one way or the other. However, it is not the end of the world."

"Joseph did a lot for me and my family. He treated me like a princess, but my despicable behaviour has truly vindicated his father. He kept on warning Joseph not to trust me and they fought over it many times. Now look what I have done to him!"

"But is Joseph aware of this?"

"Well, I am not certain but surely he would have read the letter by now? Initially I thought he somehow knew but later I realised that he didn't. While we were in the Maldives, in the beginning he was a bit sharp with me and had a short temper, and he was more of friend than a husband. Whenever I ask him something simple, he would be specific and straight to the point. Our conversation was very formal, like when you talk to your boss or a scientist. He was busy with books and his laptop. Then we had a quick chat about it and somehow I managed to trigger his old personality back to life, but not before he made chilling remarks that a cheater deserves to be strangled on their death bed. That really frightened me. Otherwise I would have confessed to him there and then."

"He talks gibberish. I beg your pardon; are you really suggesting that Joseph has never laid his hands on other women before? I bet you anything even your father-in-law has cheated on his wife, at least once or even more."

"Indeed he has. Someone saw him visiting a massage parlour. I was going to hire a private detective to get the evidence but it was too expensive, plus Joseph wouldn't like to see his father's dirty laundry in the public domain. I know Joseph, it would crush him. When his dad found out that I was pregnant he was extremely delighted about it, and oddly now he is my best friend in the family. He has single-handedly sponsored our entire holiday to the Maldives and Thailand and he is genuinely excited that soon he will be a grandpa, but the child may not even be Joseph's!" And she burst into tears again.

"You are not alone in this, Grace! One of our high school teachers says that one in every four fathers is raising a child which is not his. So a high proportion of the world population were born out of wedlock. I could be one of them and you could be one of them! Who knows, Grace? These men are disgusting. They tell you one thing and then behind your back they do something totally different.

You cry when they preach at you and then the next minute they jump in a taxi and have a fun with a madam in a massage parlour. Joseph's dad is no exception. I don't blame you. You were under monumental pressure to get pregnant at any cost and look what happened. He is the bad one and not you."

"Tell me more about Benjamin and Franklin."

"Well Franklin is a mixed race guy from Caribbean and he looks exactly like Bob Marley," said Grace. "He is the type of guy that you would like date. He was funny and charismatic; he was a guitarist who entertained people at our hospitality department in the hotel. However, he was really humble and kind, and he likes to make people laugh. He was a good listener who respects everyone's opinion. He jokes that if I was not married, he would have married me and taken me back to the Caribbean.

About Benjamin, I have to be honest with you, Precious, I don't know much about him. His accent sounded Italian, he had a British passport, but he is Danish. Talking about him now makes me feel very cheap. That guy was everything that I hate. We hardly talked to each other. He was only good at one thing: you know what I mean. He could have been a secret service agent or a drug dealer. He wouldn't talk to anyone about his business; and all that he did was read, read, read. I could never get eye contact with him. Often he would arrive at the hotel in a black cab after 1 a.m."

"Did you tell your mum about it?"

"Darling, over my dead body! She would behead me and chop me into pieces. No, I didn't tell her, and I won't."

"I think you should tell her, otherwise it will be just matter of time until she hears this from someone else! I wasn't going to tell you this, but you've been honest with me, so I will. Fiona has being spreading this rumour in town for many weeks now, and it has been spreading like wild fire. People don't buy her story because we all know what she is like. You better tell your mum about it."

"You are right, that prostitute would do anything to make my life harder. You know what she did recently? She bought a tiny book called The Way to Wealth, by Benjamin Franklin, and she gave it to my younger sister as a gift. When I confronted her about it, she said to me 'Oh your sister is helping to run your business and that book is really good for business people like you. I bought it and I decided to give it to her because she loves reading books and you don't read.' What rubbish! I hope that one day she will have cancer. And I really mean that." Again Grace burst into tears.

"Just be careful of her. She is not your friend!"

"I swear on my life that I will never talk to her again. Precious, will you come with me to my mum's tomorrow so I can tell her what has happened? I am extremely weak and I don't have any energy left. I really need your support. My mum will be really upset."

"I don't need to be there. It will be an emotional moment for both of you. This is really a sensitive matter which should be kept private for the sake of your child. I am sure she will tell you off but she won't hurt you."

"She says we have to visit that African psychic the day after tomorrow. I will wait until we come back. Or maybe I could tell her over the weekend? What do you think?"

"I think you should tell her as soon as possible. What would happen if that psychic found out and revealed it to your mum?"

"How would a psychic know that Joseph is not the real father of my unborn child?"

"People don't have to be psychic to work out what you are hiding! We can tell something is wrong by your body language. You may not be aware of it but you are unusually emotional. I thought you didn't believe that kind of psychic rubbish. Why start now?"

"When we were going on holiday a few weeks ago he gave an amulet to my mum as protection. When I started to have nightmares in the Maldives, I wore that amulet and the nightmares stopped."

Also while we were in Thailand, we met a strange old man in Bangkok. He was eccentric like Michael Jackson and looked strikingly similar, and he wore a cowboy costume. He would turn up suddenly in the middle of the hot afternoon and he would play his guitar for a while. Through playing that guitar and singing, he would tell you exactly what your problems were as if he was reading it from a script. People would queue in long line to meet him. Then all of sudden he would stop and jump into one of those bicycle taxis and then he would disappear into bustling Bangkok. Nobody knows for certain where he lives or when he will just turn up. Joseph was eager to find out from this guy whether our business would be thriving or not, and also he wanted to know more about Danjoo. We waited in the queue and there were just two people before us but the guy jumped on the taxi and then disappeared again. Strangely he wouldn't take any more than a few coins for his service.

If you gave him too much money, he would yell at you and complain that he was rich and he didn't need anything from anyone. Then angrily he would return the money back to you. A woman lost her mobile phone without realising, and she only learns about it when he told her through his guitar. She checked her handbag but the phone wasn't there. She gave him some money but he wouldn't take it. I don't know his real name but people called him Papa Charley."

"You have vindicated your mother's advice. Often she would complain to you that you thought that you knew everything, but you didn't. Sometimes in life you don't know something until you experience it."

"Precious, I have to go now, it is getting late. Where are you going on honeymoon?"

"Well, you know how Stuart loves wild animals? Our honeymoon will be in Cape Town, and after one week we will go to Botswana on safari."

"Oh, shall I come along?" Grace joked.

"Why not, let's go to Africa and have fun!" Precious laughed.

***

Joseph's mother and father were frustrated.

"Merry, I cannot get my head around why Joseph left his pregnant wife behind and disappeared into the wilderness. We haven't heard from him for two weeks now. I feel sorry for Grace. It is awful to see her in such a state. What is matter with him?" raged Vladimir.

"Please don't be a nuisance, dear! Give them some breathing space. This is how they like to live their life. Why won't you leave them alone?"

"You know that if Joseph fails, I will be blamed for it. I can't take that risk any more. I did everything for these kids: free food, free rent, free transport, and a free holiday. I gave them the opportunity to thrive, and they just want more. If the idiot fails to turn up by next week, I will ask

Grace to go back home. I can't handle these psychopaths any more."

11

Grace eventually plucked up her courage and went to talk to her mother.

"Mum, when I was a little girl you used to tell me 'humans set the rules but it is God who decides and dictates those rules'. Is that right?"

"That's right, Grace. Perfect."

"Mum, you've set so many good examples for me and my sister and you've always encourages us to be as good as we can be. But God dictates otherwise. If someone told you that your beloved daughter Grace was a prostitute, you would be heartbroken but if I admit that I am one, surely you appreciate that it is the will of God. Am I right or wrong?"

"What are you trying to say, Grace? I am confused."

Grace opened the jar which contained the story of Benjamin and Franklin and then she threw it in the front of Karen. "I have not being faithful to Joseph and he might not be the father of my child."

"Grace, why didn't you tell me about this earlier?! Regardless of his father's nasty behaviour towards you, nothing justified your action. Joseph is a gentleman and he does not deserve this. And who are Benjamin and Franklin?"

"I can't tell you anything about Benjamin, it makes me feel sick and cheap. Franklin was just a mistake. Joseph is the best. And that is all I can share with you."

"But why you haven't confessed to Joseph about it and come clean?"

"I hinted about it in the Maldives and as I was trying to elaborate, his face went pale and he stared at me like a wild beast. His eyes were popping out with rage, then he said that cheaters should be strangled and suffocated to death. He could have cut me into pieces and thrown me in the ocean, then I wouldn't be here talking about it today!"

"Grace, what else do you expect from your husband?!" Karen yelled.

"I wrote him a long letter about all of it, and I sincerely apologised for my disgusting behaviour. I confessed everything and hoped that when he read it he would forgive me, and if not then I would die in my sleep. However I asked him not to read it until when he rescued Danjoo from the jungle. I haven't heard from him for weeks now, and I am not sure whether he read it or not. I don't know what he is thinking."

"It was a terrible mistake to write him a letter. You should have confessed to him. If I were in your shoes, I would have done it that way. It is no longer about you or Joseph, it is about your unborn child. You don't want to damage that child's future. That letter is a perfect weapon which Joseph could use to ruin that child's future! If the child is not Joseph's, he will be able to use that letter as evidence of your infidelity. Do you really believe that Joseph would keep your secret for eternity? I don't think so! You did all this without thinking.

The psychic told me that you had a dark secret, but I was not expecting something so terrible. This is not cheating, it is actually madness. I am not entirely surprised, because I carried you in my stomach for nine months and I could feel that something like this would happen. I knew somehow you would be a revolutionary but in fact now you are a revolutionary sinner."

"Mum, please be kind to me. I was under immense pressure from everyone to get pregnant before our first anniversary. You know that I have never been a sinner before! This child in my womb is like a suicide vest wrapped around my waist."

"No matter what I said today, you are still my beloved daughter, Grace. I don't hate you and I will never do so. I am devastated as you. I am not sure how we will be judged when this becomes public knowledge They say that every action has consequences but also everything happens for a reason. Benjamin and Franklin is a good combination. He was a noble man who fought for independence. I will never allow you to give this child away for adoption and I care less about what people think. I will call him The Honourable Benjamin Franklin, a revolutionary who came to make a difference for mankind. And I will bring him up as a noble man and one day he will rule the world from the East to the West, as predicted by my African psychic. Human beings create rules and God decides their fate."

Dorisa and Fiona continued to spread the rumour of Grace's infidelity but before they could carry out the sinister plot which the duo planned two weeks earlier in order to create more havoc between Grace and her father-in-law, Fiona received a devastating news from her doctor.

The constant headaches that she suffered was in fact the result of brain cancer. Fiona was now going to fight an enemy a hundred times powerful than the infidelity of her innocent friend.

And without Fiona's fire and fury, Dorisa was a mere bystander who was more concerned about her own lover's lustful behaviour than showing Grace's dirty laundry in public.

It didn't get better for Grace either. Joseph's father kicked her out and she moved back to her mother's. The old man had had enough of feeding the ego of Grace and Joseph. He didn't care what happened to Grace, Joseph and the unborn child. No one had heard from Joseph, and Grace continued to struggle.

***

A few months later, a heavily pregnant Grace was getting on very well with her mother, taking advantage of the motherly love which she had missed for so long. Her best friend Precious's wedding was just around the corner, and Grace went to see her.

"Grace, have you heard anything from Joseph yet?"

"It has been five months since I last heard from him. I called the phone number he gave me, but someone with a very funny accent kept on telling me in broken English that Joseph left for Coco a long time ago. Coco is the small village where Danjoo and his lover Mami supposedly disappeared.

I fear that upon reading my letter he was heartbroken about my lustful behaviour and he couldn't handle the pressure, then he committed suicide. That is just a theory though; I don't have any evidence. He couldn't have survived the sense of guilt and betrayal which I brought upon his family. Family reputation meant a lot to him. And I really feel wicked."

"Come on, Grace! Stop being so negative about the whole saga. Joseph would never kill himself: if he was to harm anyone, that person would be you."

"I have just been trying to get on with my life. I have a new friend called Rukhsana and she is a British Bangladeshi girl. She has been taking me to an East London mosque, and she has asked me to convert to Islam. What do you think?"

"Good on you, as long as it makes you happy, why not try it? I guess soon you will start wearing those Muslim hijabs and conform to strict rules. Would you be able to handle that, though?"

"Well am kind of getting used to rules now. My mum has been taking me to see that African guy in the Midlands every two weeks and Rukhsana also took me to attend some Islamic functions in East London which do work for charity. Overall I am pretty happy with what I am doing right now. I feel that am making a difference in other people lives too and I do really enjoy doing that.

The Imam preached about the importance of repentance and the virtues of forgiveness and straight after the mosque, I went to visit Fiona at her house with Rukhsana and she was shocked to see me. We forgave each other but I could tell that she was not coping well with her cancer. She is now living on borrowed time. Last week I went see Dorisa also and I was in her house until late at night. She is really upset about her fiancée's attitude but I don't enjoy talking about that kind of stuff any more. I have forgiven everyone and I asked forgiveness from everyone too."

"You seem very busy with religion and charity work, so who is running your business?"

"Elizabeth is dealing with that. You know that she is more internet savvy than me. She still searches online hoping to find something about Joseph but I can't be bothered about it any more."

"I bet you anything, Grace, that Joseph may have married another young girl in the Far East. Move on with your life and find someone else."

"I can't actually do that, Precious, I will be married to Joseph for eternity and nothing will ever change that."

"Do you talk to your father-in-law any more?"

"Of course I do. I cook a dinner for them every weekend and he really likes it. He can't wait to welcome my baby. For some reason he is more understanding towards me. Perhaps living together in one house was not a good idea."

"I did warn you about that but you wouldn't listen."

"Tell me, Precious, what are you going to wear on your wedding day?"

"Nothing expensive, just casual and simple. Let me show you my wedding dress." They spent some time admiring the clothes, and then Grace left.

12

After many weeks in and out of the mosque with her friend Rukhsana, finally Grace embraced Islam and became a devoted Muslim by taking the oath from the Imam.

"Grace, traditionally when somebody converts to Islam, they choose a Muslim name. Would you like to?" asked Ruhksana. "It is not compulsory though, you can keep your original name if you wish!"

"Wow, that is intriguing. What is your mother's name, Rukhsana?"

"Mom's is Khadija Bibi."

"Then if you don't mind, could I use her name please? I do really admire your mum."

"That is absolutely fine, you can use her name."

"Then call me Khadija Bibi, and not Grace any more."

"In our culture, it is a great honour to use someone's name. I am sure my mum will be delighted. Now that you are a Muslim you are just like family to all Muslims. We can pray together, we can go to the mosque together, and we can even inherit each other's property."

"I am pretty excited about my new life and I am looking forward to it. It's like being born again. I have relinquished Grace and my past like a snake sheds its skin. My life will take a new direction and I will shape a new future. However the only thing which will never change is my love and connection to Joseph. Whether he is alive or not, I am married to him for eternity."

"Obviously you and Joseph are inseparable. It is like a match made in heaven."

"Would you show me how to pray, how to fast and all the rest?"

"Yes I will show you. And tomorrow I will take you to a shop in Upton Park where you can find all the essential tools for Islam, like the holy Quran, Islamic books, prayer mats, perfumes, and Muslim dress."

"That would be lovely."

"Okay, let's do that tomorrow."

***

Around 1 p.m. on the day of Precious's wedding, the hall was almost full to capacity with guests and dignitaries. Shortly before the arrival of the bride and the groom, a heavily pregnant girl wearing full Islamic veil and dressed in black from head to toe entered the wedding hall, accompanied by two Asian women. She removed the veil from her face and started to greet people, moving from one table to another. If she hadn't had a London accent, people might have thought that it was an Arab lady who had just arrived from Saudi Arabia. They were baffled and mesmerised, caught off guard by Grace's new appearance. Nobody could believe that a person who had often rebelled against common rules would ever embrace something more challenging than a western life style. But to everyone's surprise, Grace had done it.

Grace did have something to complain about, though. "Fiona, I hate the way the usher has arranged these tables. On special days like this, friends should share the same table and celebrate together with Precious like one family. We are still friends aren't we? I will ask the usher to rearrange the tables before the bride and groom arrive."

They changed tables, as she suggested. Finally Grace, Dorisa, Fiona, and Rukhsana sat at one table, then a great conversation between the old friends began.

Grace comforted Fiona about her aggressive cancer. Then they welcomed Precious and her new husband in a spectacular fashion. They lit fireworks, and threw out white flowers, singing traditional songs and dancing like school children. The music was fantastic, the food was delicious and the drinks were plenty. The wedding celebration continued for five more hours, then Dorisa asked Grace to give a speech on their behalf.

"Asalam Alikum to everyone which means 'peace be upon everyone'. I didn't expect to be giving a speech here so kindly forgive me if I don't sound organised. I will be simple and straight to the point. Traditionally people begin a speech with 'ladies and gentlemen' but for me, it is gentlemen first, isn't it?"

The crowd burst into applause.

"Joseph and I tried to revolutionize the institution of marriage by defying the rules, in the favour of pleasure and excitement and in the end, we paid a heavy price for it. Precious and Stuart, I would encourage you to set an example which will not hurt you in the future. You should obey the rules of society and follow them accordingly. Rules are here for a reason and if every person wants to live by his or her own rules, the world would be a miserable place.

I remember the words of my late father, who said that every youth is a potential rebel but the more they grow wise, the more they lean to the right and become conservative. I am the living embodiment of that. Teenage rebellion is normal in society but it wouldn't be wise to die a rebel. Gentlemen and ladies, we are gathered here today not only to celebrate the love and companionship of two individuals but also to celebrate the union of two humble families. Therefore, Precious and Stuart, you should recognise that the stronger your companionship is, the stronger the bond between your families. When I was married, my mum kept on saying that I must be loyal to my husband always, but I would be a hypocrite if I repeated that here today. Instead I would encourage you to be honest with each other, and never allow yourself to be mere husband and wife. You must strive to be the strength of one another in all your human affairs.

Please remember that in every partnership, people are bound to make mistakes, and it is inevitable that you will make some. To learn how to forgive each other is crucial to your survival as couple. I have read the holy Bible many times and currently I am studying the holy Quran. I was pleased to discover that 93 out of 99 attributes of God are about forgiveness, love, compassion, tolerance, peace, happiness, giving, sharing, understanding, and obedience to one another. Stuart and Precious, if you live by these rules, surely you will live in peace and harmony, and in the end you will die together as the happiest couple. But on your honeymoon in the jungle of Botswana, do not get lost in the forest, otherwise I will jump on the next flight to look for you, just like Joseph did.

"And finally it is my pleasure to inform you that I have decided to embrace Islam as my religion. My Muslim name is Khadija Bibi. However, whether you call me Khadija or Grace, whatever you prefer is fine by me."

She received a standing ovation, which went on for a few minutes.

"In conclusion, let's pray that somehow Fiona will find a cure for her cancer. Kindly remember me and Joseph in your prayers. You can rest assured that I have no grudge against anyone and I have forgiven everyone who might have offended me in the past and equally I am seeking your forgiveness. May God bless the newly wedded couple and may he bless you all."

***

Two weeks after Precious's wedding, Khadija went into labour and she was rushed to the Royal London Hospital. She was bleeding profusely, and tragically, after arriving in the hospital she fell into a coma. Doctors removed the child from her womb by caesarean section. It was a healthy baby boy, as predicted by her mother. Khadija was in a critical condition and shortly after dawn, Khadija Bibi died in her sleep. It was the fulfilment of her wishes.

Karen wept and wouldn't let her go, and it took a long while to adequately comfort her. A doctor brought the registration certificate for the child.

"Madam, we need to register the child's birth. Do you have a name in mind?"

"I thought we might give him the name of Honourable Benjamin Franklin but his mother and father overrode my decision. Instead they want to call him Danjoo A Miracle Child. I wouldn't do anything contrary to that wish. Therefore his name will be Danjoo A Miracle Child. Grace is his mother and Joseph is his father!

I believe that it is a sign from God. First a rebellious kid, then an obedient daughter, later a loving wife and a devoted Muslim. All this has happened for a reason. Grace became everything which she hated. Yet what she experienced in the 23 years that she lived is equal to someone who lived 1000 years. Perhaps experience is the best teacher. Humans create the rules but God decides their fate."

***

Finally, I dropped the Scottish man who told this fascinating story to me at Perry Barr in Birmingham. He threw five hundred pounds in fifty pound notes at me then he whispered "Sir, that is your tip. Good night." He walked straight into a beautiful big house, as a member of the Rothschild family would walk into a mansion in the countryside. I wondered what he was doing, in such bad weather, so late at night. Was he the house owner? Was he visiting someone else?

After such a mind-boggling story, I was emotional and overwhelmed. I sat in my car for a while then I asked myself the following questions: who was right and who was wrong? Was it justified to put such monumental pressure on those innocent lovers? Did Joseph and Grace fall on their own sword? Was it a consequence of a backward culture? Why did she die so suddenly? Was it because Joseph didn't forgive her? Is Joseph actually alive and what will happen to Danjoo? Will Joseph ever get to know the truth?

Anyway, I will try to find out.

Printed in the United States
by Baker & Taylor Publisher Services